The Way Things
Never Were

The Way Things

Norman H. Finkelstein

ACKNOWLEDGMENTS

I am grateful to the many librarians and archivists who assisted me in locating relevant information. I also wish to thank Jonathan Buckwold, M.D., for help with medical statistics, Michael Kort for his careful reading of the manuscript, and the following for sharing reminiscences: Carolyn Bishop, Iris Feldman, Mark Jacobson, John Lamb, and Joanne Shorser-Gentile. As always, I deeply appreciate the ongoing support and advice of my wife, Rosalind, and my children, Jeffrey, Jennifer, Robert, and Risa.

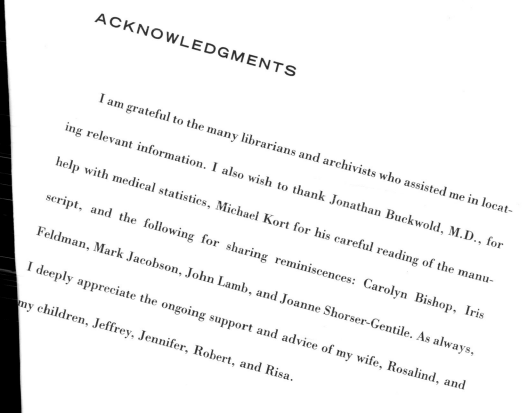

ere

McLean County Unit #5
105 - Carlock

BOOKS FOR YOUNG READERS

Atheneum Books for Young Readers
An imprint of Simon & Schuster Children's Publishing Division
1230 Avenue of the Americas
New York, New York 10020
Text copyright © 1999 by Norman H. Finkelstein
All rights reserved, including the right of reproduction in whole or in part in any

BOOK DESIGN BY NINA BARNETT

The text of this book is set in Bodoni Book

Printed in the United States of America
10 9 8 7 6 5 4 3 2 1
Library of Congress Cataloging-in-Publication Data
Finkelstein, Norman H.
The way things never were: the truth about the "good old days" / by Norman H.
Finkelstein.—1st ed.   p.   cm.
Includes bibliographical references and index.
Summary: A history of the United States during the 1950s and 1960s including
sections on health care, eating habits, family life, environmental issues, and the
condition of the elderly.
ISBN 0-689-81412-7
1. United States—History—1953–1961—Juvenile literature.
2. United States—History—1961–1969—Juvenile literature.
3. United States—History—1945–1953—Juvenile literature.
4. United States—Social conditions—1945– —Juvenile literature. [1. United States—
History—1953–1961. 2. United States—History—1961–1969. 3. United States—
History—1945–1953. 4. United States—Social conditions—1945–] I. Title.
E835.F48   1999   973.92—dc21   98-15412

Grateful acknowledgment is made to Albert Whitman and Company for the use of a
quotation from *Small Steps: The Year I Got Polio* by Peg Kehret. Copyright © 1996
by Peg Kehret.

The photo on page 89 is from *The New We Work and Play, the New We Come and Go*
by William S. Gray, A. Sterl Artley, and May Hill Arbuthnot, illustrated by Eleanor
Campbell. Copyright © 1951 by Scott, Forsman and Company. Reprinted by
permission of Addison Wesley Educational Publishers, Inc.

ents

vi

1

ments 2

17

People Were Healthier

: Pass the Pot Roast, Please

: We Could Breathe the Air

4: Home, Sweet Home

5: We Never Locked Our Doors

6: See the USA in Your Chevrolet

7: We Respected Our Elders

8: Golden Childhood

gue

s

ther Reading

ex

For Tova Meira Finkelstein

PROLOGUE

"When I was your age, I'd walk fifteen miles to school every day. And during the winter, the snow was up to my shoulders. They had winters back then! We loved it!"

Sound familiar? Since the dawn of history, adults have been telling young people how good and uplifting life used to be. And young people have always smiled and wondered: Was life so much better back then? Were the "good old days" really that good?

The good old days of the 1950s and 1960s were not a happy, carefree time for everyone in America. Overshadowing the memories of a simpler life were such overwhelming problems as the Cold War, the expansion of the suburbs, and the fear of imminent nuclear destruction.

It was a world of limited choices—of black-and-white television and white bread. Today, talk-show hosts, politicians, and others tell us how much happier we would be if only we returned to the values, lifestyle, and practices of America's past. From prayer in the schools to the reestablishment of orphanages, memories of the good old days are never far from our thoughts.

Return with us now to those good old days. Here are some truths about them.

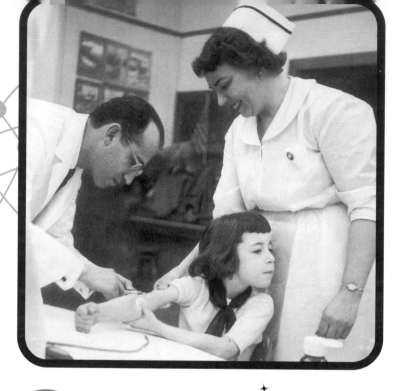

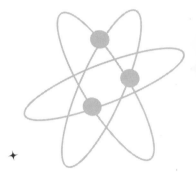

When Dr. Jonas Salk developed a polio vaccine, parents around the nation breathed a sigh of relief. The vaccine came into widespread use in 1955 after two years of testing. *National Archives*

① People Were Healthier

For many people who grew up in the 1950s and 1960s, health care was symbolized by the image of a kind and caring family doctor. He—the doctor was usually a man—thought nothing of making odd-hour house calls to examine a feverish child or reassure an arthritic aging adult. While the image is warm and comforting, it does not reflect reality. It must be noted that the haggard but kindly physician generally worked alone, depended on his own skill, and was limited to the medical knowledge of the time.

Doctors and their house calls could not provide patients with the benefits of today's advances in medical technology. Did you have a bad cold? Smelly gunk on your chest and inhaled steam might make you feel better. There were no decongestants or nonprescription painkillers except for aspirin. No one then realized that aspirin could be dangerous to children; ibuprofen and acetaminophen had not yet been created as substitutes. Sophisticated X-ray technology, such as CAT scans and MRIs, did not yet exist to provide doctors with detailed looks into the human body. Up to 15 percent of all Americans back then rated their own health as "fair or poor." While doctors could offer patients only limited help in comparison with today, they could also not adequately protect their patients from fear.

"Stay away from crowds!" "Don't go swimming!" "No, you can't go to Jimmy's birthday party!" During summer months through the mid-1950s, parents cast a wary eye on their children. What should have been a time of fun and frolic was also a time of great fear. As parents monitored children's activities, the whisper of polio was never far away. With disease in the air, schools cancelled graduations and parents kept children away from crowds and told them not to drink from public water fountains.

Polio, or infantile paralysis, is mainly a crippler of children. The virus that causes the disease is transmitted by direct exposure to an infected person. It affects the central nervous system, often paralyzing limbs or shutting down the breathing process. It was common to see young people with shriveled or lame legs wearing metal braces for support or a specially built thick-soled shoe to compensate for one leg that was shorter than the other.

In the 1950s, newspapers and magazines regularly printed frightening photographs of polio-stricken children encased in the "iron lungs" that artificially

The family doctor did everything from surgery to physicals in the office in his home (with double doors for privacy). Most often we saw him as he bustled in, cheeks pink from cold. He snapped open his black bag full of intriguing instruments, and here he practiced true bedside manner and usually left us pink pills in a flap-cornered envelope. We never knew what the pills were, just took them obediently and just as obediently recovered! These were not the days of the informed consumer.

—Carolyn Bishop

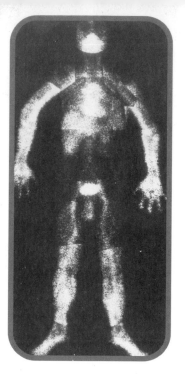

Wilhelm Roentgen received the Nobel Prize for Physics in 1901 for discovering the existence of X rays. Since then, advances in the use of X rays have resulted in truly amazing ways of accurately looking into the human body. For many years the uses of X rays were limited to traditional problem areas such as diseased lungs, broken bones, kidney stones, and skeletal and nervous system problems. Then, in the 1960s, ultrasound technology began to supplement X rays for the study of body organ functions. It was particularly useful with pregnant women to determine the well-being of the unborn baby. In the 1970s, computerized axial tomography (CAT scans) allowed cross-sectional imaging of the body. In the 1980s, thanks to advances in computers, magnetic resonance imaging (MRI) provided even clearer three-dimensional looks into the human body. Nuclear radiology, as shown in this photograph, allowed physicians to explore the workings of the human body. *National Library of Medicine*

maintained their breathing. The machine exerted a push-pull motion on the chest, allowing lungs to inhale and exhale. Not all children with polio required the use of an iron lung; some cases were worse than others. The writer Peg Kehret recalls sharing a hospital room with another polio patient. "Tommy's iron lung," she wrote, "made a swoosh, swoosh noise as it helped him breathe. I found the sound soothing and went to sleep that night pretending I was in a log cabin on a lake, listening to waves lapping the shore. In the morning I lay quietly, trying to match my breathing to the rhythmic swooshing of the iron lung. As I did, I welcomed each breath I took, grateful that it could enter my lungs without assistance." [1]

Decades of intensive research by scientists and physicians finally resulted in the discovery of effective antipolio vaccines. By the end of 1955, seven million American schoolchildren had received injections of the vaccine developed by Dr. Jonas Salk. Although the children winced at the sight of the needle, their parents were grateful to witness the end of a dreaded illness. The chairman of the American Medical Association called it "one of the greatest events in the history of medicine." An oral polio vaccine developed by Dr. Albert Sabin was given a government license in

The iron lung was an artificial respirator that allowed polio patients with respiratory paralysis to breathe and stay alive. The iron lung worked by exerting a push-pull motion on the chest. During the polio epidemic of the 1940s and 1950s the image of patients, usually children, encased in the large metal tanks was a constant reminder of the disease, which could strike anyone at any time. *National Library of Medicine*

1963. Since the 1970s, the United States and Western Europe have been polio free, although the disease still affects thousands in underdeveloped parts of the world.

Today's medical practices could have proven useful to polio patients of the 1950s. The confining iron lung would have been replaced by a simple plastic tube connected to a small portable ventilator. Physical therapy techniques could have prevented the contraction of muscles. According to one therapist, "Iron lung patients could have been up and walking instead of being totally immobilized."[2]

Even as polio became only a bad memory, other health threats haunted Americans. Measles, mumps, and scarlet fever were scourges of childhood. Ninety percent of all children prior to the mid-1960s "caught the measles." The discovery of the antimeasles vaccine in 1963 quickly lowered the incidence of the disease.

Vaccines against other dangerous infections such as diptheria and whooping cough made mothers rest easier. Public health officials had the difficult job of convincing parents to have their children immunized. In the mid-1950s, newspaper and radio advertisements urged parents to visit health clinics or doctors. In New York, one advertising campaign targeted at parents proclaimed, "One Shot and Measles Bites the Dust."[3]

But not all parents either knew or cared about the importance of these vaccinations for their young children. Vaccine protection for thousands of children was regularly ignored by many.

Poliomyelitis affected a person's central nervous system and often resulted in paralysis. Although it mainly affected children, adults were not immune. Physical therapy was one important way polio patients worked to regain at least partial use of affected limbs. Exercising in a pool made such therapy easier. *National Library of Medicine*

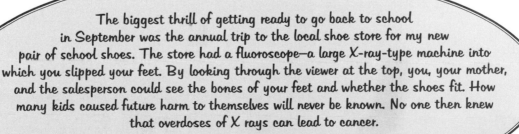

The biggest thrill of getting ready to go back to school in September was the annual trip to the local shoe store for my new pair of school shoes. The store had a fluoroscope—a large X-ray-type machine into which you slipped your feet. By looking through the viewer at the top, you, your mother, and the salesperson could see the bones of your feet and whether the shoes fit. How many kids caused future harm to themselves will never be known. No one then knew that overdoses of X rays can lead to cancer.
—Norman Finkelstein

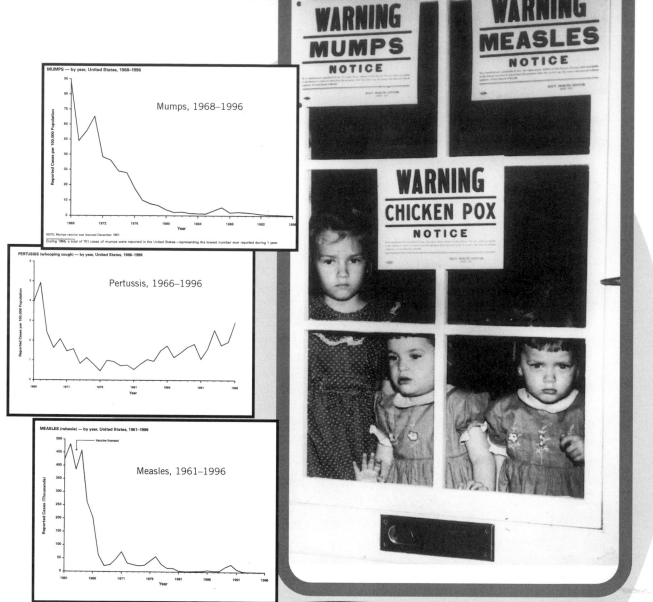

MUMPS — by year, United States, 1968–1996

Mumps, 1968–1996

Reported Cases per 100,000 Population

NOTE: Mumps vaccine was licensed December 1967.
During 1996, a total of 751 cases of mumps were reported in the United States—representing the lowest number ever reported during 1 year.

PERTUSSIS (whooping cough) — by year, United States, 1966–1996

Pertussis, 1966–1996

Reported Cases per 100,000 Population

Year

MEASLES (rubeola) — by year, United States, 1961–1996

Vaccine licensed

Measles, 1961–1996

Reported Cases (Thousands)

Year

Centers for Disease Control and Prevention

Medicine's Greatest Journeys: 100 Years of Healing by Smolan and Moffit, Little, Brown, 1992

WARNING MUMPS NOTICE

WARNING MEASLES NOTICE

WARNING CHICKEN POX NOTICE

1953—I remember being in first grade at P.S. 165 in Queens, New York. The minute I walked through the door and smelled the antiseptic alcohol, I knew it was polio vaccine day. The cafeteria was temporarily turned into a medical center. We were called down class by class and nervously lined up for our shots. We were given buttons which read: "I AM A POLIO PIONEER," and I saved mine for years. Our school was part of an early testing program. At some point, our parents received letters informing them if we had been given the real vaccine or the "water" (as we called it). Those of us unlucky enough to be given the water had to go through the vaccination process all over again, this time with the real thing.

—Iris Feldman

"Vaccines work," said Dr. David Satcher, the director of the Centers for Disease Control (CDC). "They are superb, cost-effective tools to prevent disease. However, parents can't be sure their child is fully protected until they check. We encourage parents and health care providers to stop and check a child's shot record at every medical visit."[4]

Today, there are ten diseases, including measles, mumps, rubella, chicken pox, and hepatitis, that can be prevented through vaccination. The difficulty lies in helping parents keep up with all the new vaccines and getting their children vaccinated on time to give them protection from disease. A step in the right direction is a combination vaccine for measles, mumps, and rubella so children no longer have to endure individual shots and their parents do not have to keep complicated records.

By 1996, thanks to the cooperation of public health agencies, private businesses, and community educational groups, the government could proudly announce that childhood vaccination goals were exceeded. More than 90 percent of all toddlers receive the most critical doses of the majority of the routinely recommended vaccines for children by age two. Government programs make certain that all children, rich and poor, have access to medical attention. In 1965, 20 percent of children whose family income was below the poverty level had never been examined by a physician. By 1970, that number had dropped to 8 percent. Today, the infant death rate in the United States has dropped to an all-time low. Dr. Satcher proudly stated, "The investments we have made in education and prevention programs are paying real dividends."[5]

Tuberculosis, or TB, is a lung disease which is spread through the air from one person to another. It thrives in crowded, closed places. Although the risk to most people is low, once contracted, TB is a serious disease. Years ago, a TB patient would have had to be hospitalized in a special hospital for months or even years. Educating people to avoid long-term crowded living and working conditions used to be the only way to curb the spread of the disease. Today, TB can be controlled with a variety of drugs. *Medicine's Greatest Journeys: 100 Years of Healing* by Smolan and Moffit, Little, Brown, 1992

Elderly Americans have also demonstrated a growing appreciation of the benefits of vaccination. They are prime targets for the consequences of flu and pneumonia, often fatal diseases for people over the age of sixty-five. Pneumonia, which often results from flu, is the fifth leading cause of death among the elderly. Experts estimate that up to 80 percent of deaths from the flu could be prevented with a flu shot. "A simple flu shot," a government doctor said, "often turns out to be a life-saver for many frail elderly people and helps avoid needless suffering and unnecessary medical costs."[6] By 1995, 58 percent of the nation's elderly received annual flu shots. Just eight years earlier, that figure stood at 32 percent. Vaccinations against pneumonia have also increased.

The life expectancy of a baby born in 1940 was sixty-three years. It jumped to sixty-eight in the 1960s and continued to increase until, in the 1990s, it reached seventy-five. What caused the rise? Some factors that contributed to longer life include the widespread availability of affordable healthy foods, a diminishing number of smokers, increased physical activity, and better medical care. Heart and kidney transplants, CAT scans, coronary bypass surgery, and advances in drug therapies have extended lives.

Prior to the widespread availability of antibiotics in the late 1940s and early 1950s, ordinary childhood infections often resulted in death. Aspirin and home remedies had little effect on meningitis, scarlet fever, or strep throat. Yellow or red "quarantine"

If you had a life-threatening emergency up until the 1970s, the only thing you could hope for was a quick and uneventful trip to the hospital. Chances were that the ambulance contained no lifesaving equipment or highly trained personnel. Today's ambulances are usually filled with high-tech equipment designed to keep patients alive on the trip to the hospital. The ambulance in this photograph dates back to the 1960s, when technical medical equipment began to be built in. Today, ambulances are usually staffed by trained paramedics who are in constant touch with nurses and doctors at the hospital emergency room. *Library of Congress*

We went to the beach a lot as a family during the summer.
It was a twenty-minute ride by trolley. One Sunday evening, after a full day of fun
in the sun, my father announced he did not feel well and went to bed. By the next morning,
he was feeling worse. His head hurt and he felt so dizzy, he could not stand up. His body ached.
My mother called the police. The city owned one ambulance, operated by the police. It looked very
much like a hearse only painted gray with a police light on top. Two burly officers put my father on
a stretcher and carried him downstairs to the ambulance. My mother got in with my father, and the
ambulance sped off, its siren screaming for the ten-minute drive to the hospital. Fortunately, he just
had a bad case of sunstroke and after treatment was sent home. Today, as I look back, I realize
how unprepared the ambulance service was. The officers had little, if any, medical training.
They were body carriers. The ambulance contained no lifesaving equipment.
There was no communication with the hospital in the event medical
aid was needed during the trip.

—Norman Finkelstein

signs on front doors in their neighborhoods warned visitors to stay away—someone inside had been diagnosed with an infectious disease. Other "magic bullet" drugs lowered the death rates of scourge diseases such as tuberculosis and pneumonia. Not so long ago, removal of a diseased gallbladder resulted in a patient spending a week or more in a hospital. Today, advances in surgical treatment mean that many gallbladder patients go home the same or the next day.

The death rates for people from heart disease, stroke, diabetes, and even accidents decreased dramatically between the 1950s and the 1990s. The death rate from heart disease dropped from 440 people per 100,000 deaths in 1960 to 342 in 1985. In many ways, the war against heart disease is being won. Such lifesaving procedures as balloon angioplasty and bypass surgery were not widely available just a few decades ago. Neither were some of the truly remarkable heart drugs or the knowledge that diet does affect the heart.

Back in the 1950s or 1960s, scientists were not totally convinced that a high-fat diet clogged arteries and contributed to heart attacks and strokes. By the 1990s, there was little doubt. Today, patients who have had one heart attack have access to new drugs that lower cholesterol levels and can protect them from a second and possibly fatal attack.

Years ago, when a person was wheeled into an emergency room complaining of chest pains, a doctor

Life expectancy at birth:

1940	1990
62.9 years	75.4 years

Source: National Center for Health Statistics, CDC.

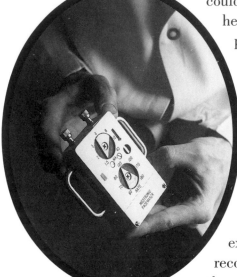

Patients with abnormally low heart rates can suffer from dizziness, weakness, palpitations, shortness of breath, or fainting. Sometimes a symptom could lead to death. Since 1958, hundreds of thousands of people have literally been given new lives by having a pacemaker implanted in their bodies. It automatically regulates the heart's rhythm. Over the years, pacemakers have become much smaller than the one pictured here, and much more sophisticated. Over 100,000 new patients a year benefit from this lifesaving invention. *Library of Congress*

could not quickly determine whether the pain was from a heart attack or merely the result of eating too much pepperoni pizza. Today, new radiologic imaging techniques, tailored to the patient's symptoms, can economically diagnose heart problems right in the emergency room and lead to fast, lifesaving treatment. If the pizza were at fault, the doctor can simply prescribe an antacid and send the patient home. Not only does the hospital save hundreds of dollars in unnecessary tests, but the patient's stress level is automatically reduced.

The statistics on cancer deaths, however, show a marked increase during the last forty years. Some experts say that this is due to heightened awareness in recognizing cancer's symptoms. Also, as people live longer, there is more time for cancers to develop. But on the positive side, new innovations in drug therapy and radiology greatly increase the life spans of many cancer patients. In fact, beginning in 1990, the National Cancer Institute (NCI) discovered a decline in the cancer death rate in the United States. This was attributed to the strides that were made in prevention through a decrease in smoking and early detection and treatment of the disease.

The new medical technology is nothing short of amazing. Years ago, cancer patients did not have much hope. The widespread use of radiation and chemotherapy changed the cancer survival rate. A problem with the conventional radiation therapy of the past was that it not only killed cancer cells, but also damaged surrounding healthy tissue. Today, cancer scientists are studying the use of proton beam technology originally designed for use in nuclear physics research. They believe that the proton beam can deliver 50 percent more tumor-killing radiation

"The recent drop in the cancer death rate marks a turning point from the steady increases we have seen throughout much of the century. The 1990s will be remembered as the decade when we measurably turned the tide against cancer."

—Richard Klausner, M.D.
Director of the NCI,
November 14, 1996

to the cancer with 70 percent less damage to surrounding tissue. The advantages, according to Dr. Herman Suit, chairman of radiation oncology at Harvard Medical School in Boston, are "increased survival . . . and increased likelihood of survival without complications."[7]

For hundreds of years, people attributed the stomach pain and discomfort of some peptic ulcers to stress. Eating bland food was thought to control the symptoms. A typical lunch for a peptic ulcer sufferer in the 1950s was a bowl of plain crackers in milk. In 1985, scientists discovered that the real cause of peptic ulcers was a bacteria. Studies showed that 60 percent of Americans are infected by the bacteria and that 25 million will develop ulcers during their lifetime. When antibiotics were prescribed to control the disease, patients were able to eat regular foods again.

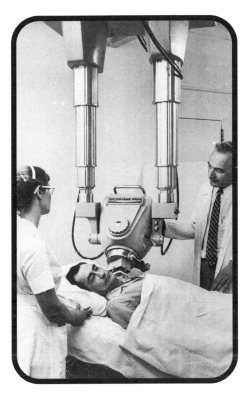

To diagnose ailments or attack cancers, radiologists are now able to focus powerful radiation beams on tumors. In this 1962 photograph, a doctor and technician check equipment before administering Cesium 137, a by-product of research in atomic energy. The chemical is used to treat cancer beneath the surface of the skin. *National Archives*

In the fifties and sixties it seemed that nearly every adult was smoking cigarettes. Actually, in 1965, 42 percent of all adults smoked. By 1994, that figure was down significantly to 25 percent. Between 1976 and 1995, daily smoking by high school seniors dropped from around 36 to 29 percent.

In the late 1950s, famous newscaster Edward R. Murrow was hardly ever seen on or off camera without a cigarette between his fingers. His son recalls being sent out to a local store to buy several cartons at a time for his father. Murrow died of lung cancer in 1965 at the age of fifty-seven.

Today, we are witnessing a sharp decline in cigarette smoking. Local communi-

Cigarette smoking by adults eighteen years and older:	
1965	**1994**
42.3%	25.0%

Source: National Center for Health Statistics, CDC.

ties have banned smoking in public buildings, and restaurants are either completely smoke free or have set aside specific sections for smokers. For decades, tobacco companies successfully targeted young people with eye-catching advertisements featuring famous actors and cartoon characters. "You're so smart to smoke Parliaments," one 1950s ad praised its customers.

The tobacco companies downplayed the health risks of smoking and even used doctors and health claims in their advertisements. One 1953 Chesterfield cigarette newspaper ad boasted that a medical specialist had given a group of Chesterfield smokers regular examinations every two months. He reported no adverse effects to nose, throat, and sinuses from smoking Chesterfield. Heroes and heroines in nearly every Hollywood film of that era smoked cigarettes with abandon. No one, on the screen or in the real world, seemed concerned that smoke was also being inhaled by innocent bystanders. Before the 1964 report of the surgeon general of the United States that linked smoking with serious illnesses including lung disease and cancer, only 50 percent of Americans believed that smoking was a cause of lung cancer, and only 38 percent thought it could result in heart disease. Just a few years later, those figures had climbed significantly. By the 1990s, Americans also accepted the fact that "secondhand" smoke was just as much a public health hazard.

An important factor in decreasing the number of smokers was federal government involvement in safety and health issues. Activism by the Food and Drug Administration (FDA) and the Federal Trade Commission has directly changed public opinion about smoking. Even as the surgeon general's 1964 smoking report was published, tobacco company executives downplayed the scientific news and relied on slick advertising to combat proven medical facts. The "Marlboro Country" cigarette ads marked one of the most successful advertising campaigns ever devised.

Percent of high school seniors who used alcohol, cigarettes, and marijuana:		
	1976	**1995**
Marijuana	27.1%	21.2%
Alcohol	68.2%	51.3%
Cigarettes	36.7%	29.0%

Source: "Monitoring the Future," study conducted by the University of Michigan, Institute for Social Research, 1996.

The ads depicted Marlboro Country as an unpolluted and healthy place. The tanned and handsome Marlboro Man (who in real life eventually died of lung cancer) was admired by women and envied by men. No one knows how many teenagers began smoking Marlboros in an attempt to become part of that appealing, fictional world.

The government has also played an important role in making the United States not just healthier, but safer. Americans used to rely on a hodgepodge of local, state, and federal product safety and environmental regulations. Since the 1970s, new federal agencies have been created and older agencies have become more activist. New federal laws were enacted, including the National Traffic and Motor Vehicle Safety Act, the Wholesale Meat Act, and the Radiation Control for Health and Safety Act. The result of this government intervention was a decline in work-related and highway deaths and accidents, air crashes, and even environmental pollution. America became a safer, healthier, and cleaner country.

The CDC, the Centers for Disease Control and Prevention, is one of the federal agencies charged with protecting the health of all Americans. In many ways, the center's scientists and physicians operate as detectives tracking down illness. In 1955, when polio surprisingly appeared in children who received the recently approved Salk vaccine, the CDC traced the contamination to a laboratory in California and the danger was eliminated. Two years later, the scientists tracked the course of a massive influenza epidemic for the first time. Their work led to the development of the flu vaccines in use today.

The 1950s and 1960s were the decades of the large automobile, which presented new concerns for safety. Steel and chrome were used to create vehicles that, while

When automobiles were still young, engineers looked for ways to make engines run better and without the annoying "knock" which was so common. In the 1920s scientists discovered that if they added a lead compound, tetraethyl lead, to the gasoline, car engines ran better. There was, however, a serious problem. Exposure to lead was known to be a health risk sometimes even leading to death. Nonetheless, the Surgeon General in 1925 permitted the sale of the new fuel, ruling that concentrations of lead discharged in automobile exhaust fumes would be minimal, and the dangers were far outweighed by the benefits to motorists. In the 1960s, scientific evidence made it clear that lead was a serious health hazard. Elevated levels of lead in blood cause nerve damage, anemia, or mental retardation in children. Under the direction of the Environmental Protection Agency (EPA), a 25-year program which ended in 1996 phased out the sale and use of all leaded gasoline in the United States. "The elimination of lead from gas is one of the great environmental achievements of all time," said Carol M. Browner, the EPA Administrator. *Library of Congress*

Ethyl Corporation

roomy inside, took on the outside proportions of mechanized whales. It was not until 1966 that the automobile industry was prodded to finally sacrifice style for meaningful safety. A book by a young consumer activist, Ralph Nader, got things started. *Unsafe at Any Speed* pointed an accusing finger at the industry with concrete examples of poor designs and technology. Automobile bumpers, for example, were designed for cosmetic beauty: They offered little or no protection in the event of a crash. These flaws in poorly designed auto systems often resulted in death and injury to drivers and passengers. Nader's loud call for change led to a highly publicized congressional hearing that resulted in landmark auto safety legislation.

The rise in the use of seat belts is a good example of those improved automobile safety standards. In 1963, convinced that seat belts could prevent many traffic deaths, motorists began insisting on them. Of the 65 million cars on the road then, only 8 million had seat belts. Today, seat belts, much improved in design over the past few decades, are mandatory on all automobiles sold in the United States. Automobiles are now built with padded dashes and recessed control panels. Air bags, although not without problems, help save lives. By the mid-1990s, Americans

Workplace safety has improved since it came under the scrutiny of the federal government. From a high of 14,000 dead in 1965, new safety rules have been responsible for a drop in deaths to 8,500 by 1992.

saw the number of automobile deaths dramatically decline by nearly half.

Prior to the late 1960s, lead was a common ingredient in household paint and gasoline. Human exposure to lead occurs through inhalation of air and ingestion of lead in food, soil, water, or dust. A prime source of lead poisoning was automobile exhaust systems. From the 1920s through the 1960s, leaded gasoline was the major automobile fuel. The phaseout of leaded gasoline led to a sharp decrease of airborne lead concentrations. In 1996, leaded gasoline was totally banned for sale in the United States. Lead poses a particular danger to health: It accumulates in bone tissue and causes learning problems.

Lead and other mineral wastes from factories were freely discharged into America's rivers and streams and made their way into drinking water. In communities throughout America, neighborhoods near industrial sites became aware of increased health problems such as cancer and birth defects. One resident of a Kentucky town explained that "every house here has had health problems, leukemia, birth defects, and miscarriages."[8] Stricter regulations were instituted by the federal government in a number of environmental and health initiatives including the Safe Drinking Water Act and the Clean Water Act.

Spurred to action by consumer product risks resulting in poisonings, electrocutions, burns, and other injuries, Congress created the Consumer Products Safety Commission (CPSC). In the decade from 1979 to 1988, the average rate of death and injury per 100,000 consumers decreased by 20 percent.

Before the CPSC instituted and legally enforced strict government standards, the design of many popular manufactured products caused unnecessary injury to children. Flammable sleepwear led to painful burns or even death for hundreds of children. Other children

Death rates from accidents of all kinds:

1970	1985
56.4%	19.2%

Death rates from motor vehicle accidents:

1970	1985
26.9%	19.2%

Source: U.S. Bureau of the Census, *Statistical Abstract of the United States*

were burned when they played with their parents' poorly designed cigarette lighters. Still other children died when they were able to easily open medicine bottles and swallow pills. Infants died when they were caught in crib slats that were too widely spaced.

Researchers were puzzled by the number of infants who died of suffocation in their cribs. It was not until the 1990s that research by the CPSC pinpointed high levels of carbon dioxide in crib bedding. This conclusion resulted in the recommen-dation that infants should be positioned on their backs or sides rather than on their stomachs, as was the practice until then.

Back in the 1950s and 1960s, hundreds of chil-dren were killed or maimed by defective toys. Some children swallowed small removeable game parts, which then blocked breathing; others were hurt when unsafe riding toys toppled over. Again, gov-ernmental regulations were put in place that have dramatically lowered the number of such accidents. It was only in the late 1970s that bicycle helmets came into popular use. Still, not everyone takes the government's advice about wearing them.

National health expenditures, per person:

1960	1994
$141	$3,510

Source: U.S. Bureau of the Census, *Statistical Abstract*

Westinghouse Electric Corporation

② Pass the Pot Roast, Please

America's eating habits have changed dramatically since 1950. Just after the food-rationing years of World War II, people wanted to enjoy eating again. The emphasis was on food staples such as meat, potatoes, bacon, and eggs. Few worried about cholesterol, fat, or chemical ingredients in food. The standard 1950s dinner meal consisted of meat and potatoes with all the fixings, including generous servings of butter and sour cream. Americans ate lots of protein . . . and fat! When the book *The Low Fat, Low Cholesterol Diet* appeared in 1951, its reception was less than overwhelming.

Trust Swanson

Who else gives you <u>all-beef</u> sirloin in a frozen dinner?

There's no comparison! Only a Swanson TV Brand Dinner boasts tender, juicy, all-beef sirloin like this! It's cooked with loving Swanson care, and ladled with rich brown gravy. Tender peas, too, and French fries that set a new high in crispy good flavor. Mmmm . . . for good frozen dinners, trust Swanson!

The Campbell Soup Company

Food, the old American love,

had a new competitor in the 1950s: television. But Americans, being an imaginative people, quickly searched out ways to adjust meals to the lure of the television age. In 1954, Swanson Foods introduced the first "TV dinners." These frozen meals did nothing to lower the salt and fat content of Americans' diets, but they did offer convenience. The television era also gave rise to a meteoric growth of snack and fast-food sales. Munching and crunching in front of the television became a national pastime. Few worried about the effects of a high-fat and salt-laden diet. Even as late as 1966, the official U.S. *Yearbook of Agriculture* made no mention of health dangers consumers faced from saturated fat.

In spite of our continuing love of munchies, the American diet has shown healthful improvement over the past thirty years. A study in 1965 showed large differences in dietary quality among different groups of Americans. By the 1990s, the diets of all groups had become relatively similar—and healthier. People had become more aware of the dangers posed to health by excess fat, cholesterol, and salt. Highly publicized medical studies proved a relationship between a high-fat diet and coronary heart disease. The meat-and-gravy meals of the past have been partially replaced by healthier food choices. Beef consumption in the United States decreased from 80 percent of all meat consumed in 1970 to 63 percent in 1994. And just as important, the meat we eat tends to be lower in fat—leaner and healthier than in the past.

We have also turned away from other high-fat foods. Americans have reduced the amount of whole milk they drink by choosing low-fat and nonfat milk. Studies now show that all milk contains the same nutrients; switching to 1 percent or skim milk just eliminates the fat. At the same time, there has been an increase in the amount of fish, chicken, and fresh vegetables eaten. Even the consumption of broccoli, the green vegetable once publicly avoided and ridiculed by President George Bush, has increased fourfold due in part to cancer prevention claims.

America at the midpoint of the twentieth century was a simpler place than it is today. People had fewer choices in their everyday lives. At the same time, shopping for food was more time-consuming than it is today. Frequent food shopping was a way of life for the typically homebound wife and mother of the 1950s. If the family needed bread, there was the local bakery with its special array of cakes and baked goods. Other stores specialized in fruits, vegetables, or fish. A daily stroll to the stores was an opportunity to greet friends and chat—and get out of the house.

While food shopping was a social experience, product choices were limited. The idea of "one-stop" food shopping originated

An ice-cold soda was the perfect way to cap a shopping trip downtown. Vending machines were scarce, but a thirsty shopper could always sit at the counter of the local drug store or five-and-dime department store and sip a refreshing cold drink. *The Coca Cola Company*

Host to Thirsty Main Street
Inviting you to the pause that refreshes with ice-cold Coca-Cola
5¢

in the mid-1940s with expanded grocery stores and chain supermarkets, such as the A&P, but it took decades for them to fully develop into the megamarkets of today. When supermarkets began to open, they did not immediately replace the small neighborhood grocery stores. These "mom-and-pop" stores, each usually owned and run by a single family, provided shoppers with a limited inventory of packaged and fresh foods. The local grocer was an important member of the community who knew customers by name and food preferences. There was no need to walk up and down aisles to select items in Harry's Variety Store or Anna's Corner Store. The friendly grocer behind the counter took care of your list. In many cases, you could even telephone in your food order and have it delivered.

Caitlin Van Dusen

While that personal touch in food shopping is long past, today's consumers at a typical warehouse-sized supermarket find thousands of items arrayed before them and services the corner grocer could never have imagined. There is increased availability of gourmet, specialty, and ethnic foods—everything from pâté to pizza to bagels. The cereal aisle alone contains dozens of choices, in boxes of varying size. In many of today's supermarkets, you can do your banking, drop off dry cleaning, or rent a video.

The typical supermarket produce department today carries over 400 items, up from 250 in the late 1980s and 150 in the mid-1970s. Also, the number of ethnic and gourmet foods has also increased.

—*Food Review*, May 17, 1996

Busy families like to eat at home. They just don't have the time or desire to cook. In today's supermarkets, shoppers can buy freshly made in-store rotisseried chickens and a variety of prepared side dishes and salads to take home and serve without the muss and fuss of preparation. Do you feel like having a fresh mushroom and anchovy pizza? Some supermarkets have in-store national brand pizza shops where you can order a custom-made pizza-to-go while you shop. In frozen food alone, the

United States annually consumes over 70 pounds per person of a variety of foods ranging from enchiladas to eggplant parmigiana. The staple frozen foods back in the 1950s were mixed vegetables, ice cream, and TV dinners.

Food advertisers, who had great success with targeting radio cereal advertising to children in the 1930s and 1940s, discovered the purchasing power of television early in the 1950s. In 1952, Kellogg's introduced two popular sugar cereals, Sugar Smacks and Sugar Frosted Flakes, and began targeting them to children with cartoon characters and catchy jingles. Tony the Tiger became a television personality in his own right. Soft drink companies also successfully targeted young people with clever catchphrases and advertisements. "Now, it's Pepsi, for those who think young" went one 1960s jingle.

The traditional family of the 1950s and 1960s was headed by a father who went off to work each morning and a mother who stayed home to raise the children. With the growing number of two-career families after 1970, the time available for routine home chores grew smaller. So it was not surprising that people began to eat more meals away from home. In fact, by the early 1990s, Americans were spending over 40 percent of their family food money in restaurants. At one time, eating out at a restaurant was a luxury, reserved for special occasions. But no longer.[1]

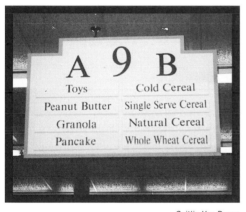

Caitlin Van Dusen

Fast-food chains such as McDonald's, Burger King, and Wendy's dot the American countryside. Their growth has been astronomical. Until they came along, the quality of food and service in fast-food restaurants varied widely. They had poor reputations for bad food and curt service. By 1995, consumers were spending more money on fast food than on meals in full-service restaurants. The number of all types of eating establishments has had similar growth, from 275,000 in 1977 to 474,000 in 1992, while the number of Americans who daily eat at least one food or beverage away from home is one-third higher today than in 1977.

The familiar golden arches of McDonald's restaurants became new landmarks in America. The fast-food explosion changed the way we eat. For the first time Americans could know in advance exactly what they would find when they entered under the arches. *McDonald's Corporation*

The health consequences of fast-food meals have long been in question. The meal your parents enjoyed at McDonald's—a Big Mac, a large order of french fries, and a large chocolate shake—contained over 45 grams of fat and 1,140 calories. You can still buy the same meal today with the slight distinction that the french fries are now probably prepared in vegetable oil rather than beef fat.

Many restaurants today try to give customers healthy alternatives that were not widely offered only a decade ago. In so doing, restaurants and fast-food outlets mirror changes in Americans' concerns for improved health. The nostalgically remembered bakeries, fruit stores, and fish shops that lined the main streets of most American towns in the 1950s and 1960s were limited not only in the number of choices, but also in the health content of the foods they offered. High-cholesterol lard has been replaced in many foods with healthier vegetable oils, and olive oil or

```
..·TO OPEN··.
KEEP REFRIGERATED
GRADE A PASTEURIZED HOMOGENIZED
FAT REDUCED FROM 8g TO 5g PER SERVING
```

Nutrition Facts
Serving Size 1 Cup (240mL)
Servings Per Container 4

Amount Per Serving	
Calories 130	Calories from Fat 45
	% Daily Value*
Total Fat 5g	8%
Saturated Fat 3g	15%
Cholesterol 20mg	7%
Sodium 130mg	5%
Total Carbohydrate 12g	4%
Dietary Fiber 0g	0%
Sugars 12g	
Protein 8g	16%

Vitamin A 10% • Vitamin C 2% • Calcium 30%
Iron 0% • Vitamin D 25%

* Percent Daily Values are based on a 2,000 calorie diet.
Your daily values may be higher or lower depending on
your calorie needs:

	Calories:	2,000	2,500
Total Fat	Less than	65g	80g
Sat. Fat	Less than	20g	25g
Cholesterol	Less than	300mg	300mg
Sodium	Less than	2,400mg	2,400mg
Total Carbohydrate		300g	375g
Dietary Fiber		25g	30g
Protein		50g	65g

Calories per gram:
Fat 9 • Carbohydrate 4 • Protein 4

**INGREDIENTS: REDUCED FAT MILK, VITAMIN A
PALMITATE, VITAMIN D3.
DISTRIBUTED BY COMPASS FOODS**

margarine is used in cooking instead of butter. Reduced-fat mayonnaise and salad dressings are also commonly available. Turkey and chicken franks with fewer calories and lower fat content can be substituted for regular hot dogs. Fish, chicken, and turkey entrées compete with steaks and chops.

Today's restaurants offer "healthy heart" menus with entrées containing small amounts of fat and reduced calories. Vegetable, tofu, and grain mixtures can be ordered in place of high-fat-content hamburgers. Lower fat deli meats such as turkey, ham, and lean roast beef are widely available. One sandwich chain offers vegetarian turkey submarine sandwiches made with a vegetable-based meat substitute. "We're not taking away any of our customers' favorite foods, we're just making them healthier, and also making lower calorie options available for customers who ask," said one of the chain's dieticians. [2]

Today, the food-service industry continues to respond to the needs of working adults and their families. Career-pressured mothers and fathers do not always have time to prepare meals at home. Convenient, value-priced food service has become a popular alternative. The response has been an increase in the sale of prepared take-home food easily warmed up in the kitchen microwave. "Typical" American meals are changing too, reflecting a growing interest in ethnic foods. In

Per capita food consumption in the United States:

Food Item	1970	1995
Red meat	131.7 lbs.	114.8 lbs.
Beef	79.6 lbs.	63.6 lbs.
Fish	11.7 lbs.	15.1 lbs.
Eggs	308.9	237.6
Butter	5.4 lbs.	4.8 lbs.
Lard	4.6 lbs.	1.7 lbs.
Fresh fruits	101.2 lbs.	126.7 lbs.
Fresh vegetables	85.4 lbs.	113.9 lbs.
Milk	31.3 gals.	24.7 gals.
Whole	25.4 gals.	9.1 gals.
Low-fat	4.4 gals	12.2 gals.
Skim	1.3 gals.	3.3 gals.

Source: U.S. Bureau of the Census, *Statistical Abstract*

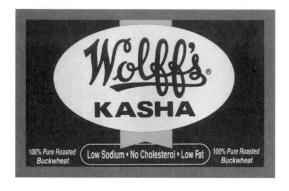

1991, salsa replaced ketchup, the most American of condiments, in sales. The concern with healthy eating styles caused manufacturers to reduce the fat and salt content of food products. This made them seem bland to some. But to put flavor back in, many food producers are turning to the international flavors found in Hispanic, Thai, and Middle Eastern cooking. How about a Thai pizza with mint, basil, and coriander, or a babaganoush sandwich on pita bread?

The cans and boxes of food bought at the neighborhood grocery used to simply indicate the contents: tuna fish, tomato soup, green peas. Although the packages were required by law to list all ingredients, they rarely indicated nutritional information. In 1994, government regulations went into effect mandating the nutritional labeling of all packaged foods. Consumers could finally easily learn and understand the health benefits (or lack thereof) for almost all of the food products they bought. Uniform definitions for terms such as *low-fat* and *high-fiber*, used differently by each manufacturer, were standardized.

Another change that affected food purchasers concerned the health and safety claims manufacturers freely made about their products. Government agencies

Ah, the smell of pickles in the barrel! Harry's Variety Store was just down the street from our house. The entire store was no larger than a classroom. Harry stood behind the counter wearing a tattered white apron. I especially remember the day Harry got his first (and only) freezer chest. The contents of that chest included two flavors of ice cream and bags of frozen vegetables. (My mother's favorite was the mixed-vegetable bag.) You had to know what you wanted when you entered the store. There was no browsing. You walked up to Harry (or his wife) and asked for a large box of cornflakes or a bottle of ginger ale. Harry only carried one brand of most items, anyway. There may not have been many choices, but there was personalized service. Did Mother run short of cash? No problem; I would just say, "Put it on the bill." At the end of the week, my parents would pay what they owed. If the family was sick, a quick telephone call would get the eggs delivered to your door. These little stores were sometimes called "variety stores," although as I look back, I don't remember much in the way of variety.

—Norman Finkelstein

became more active in assuring the safety of products. An example is saccharine, used widely as an artificial sweetener until 1972. That year, after careful scientific study by the FDA, it was removed from the list of safe food additives because it caused cancer in test animals.

Years ago, exaggerated advertising claims confused consumers and often led to purchases of ineffective or even harmful products. Today, manufacturers' claims linking a food with reducing the risk of a disease are allowed only under very specific conditions. Those claims must be phrased so that consumers can understand the relationship between the nutrient and the disease and the nutrient's importance in relationship to a daily diet. Examples of such claims are: "While many factors affect heart disease, diets low in saturated fat and cholesterol may reduce the risk of this disease" or that a product is a "good source" of dietary fiber, which may prevent cancer, or is "low-sodium," which might lower high blood pressure.

Imitation fruit drinks were very popular with children thirty and forty years ago ("How about a nice Hawaiian Punch?"). Consumers never knew the amount of real juice, if any, in these drinks. That detail was left to the discretion of the manufacturer, and the cans or bottles never contained nutritional information. Today, beverages that claim to contain juice must declare the total percentage of juice on the label.

Today's governmentally regulated food labels provide many new benefits that were unavailable to our parents and grandparents. We are more aware of what we eat and of the related benefits of exercise. By knowing the nutritional content of the foods we buy and carefully choosing what we eat, we can all benefit from decreased rates of allergic reactions to food, coronary heart disease, cancer, osteoporosis, obesity, and high blood pressure.[3]

③ We Could Breathe the Air

Airplane passengers crossing the United States in the 1950s and 1960s could always identify large cities from the air by the surrounding haze and smog. Americans breathed unhealthy air, swam in polluted rivers, and built homes on top of chemical waste sites. Concern for the environment emerged as a national movement only within the past few decades. Some people date it from 1969 and the political activity surrounding the first Earth Day when, across the country, speeches, marches, and teach-ins launched America's environmental movement. The impact on the country was tremendous, and membership in environmental organizations grew dramatically.

In the 1940s, before, during, and after World War II, and during the 1950s, factory smokestacks and automobile emissions polluted the air everyone breathed. Cities like Pittsburgh and Los Angeles were famous for the visible signs of pollution that surrounded them. Since new environmental laws were passed in the 1970s, smog in the United States has been reduced by one-third, and invisible pollution contaminants, which fell to the earth in the form of acid rain, cut nearly 50 percent.

> *I lived in a small city just outside Boston. On one end was a rubber factory, on the other a large chemical factory. Depending on which way the wind blew, I could inhale the odor of rubber or burning sulfur. You could actually see the chemical clouds moving over the city.*
> —Norman Finkelstein

Rivers throughout the country were polluted with waste discharges from factories. When people remember good times fishing and boating in the 1960s, they sometimes fail to remember that some of America's best-known waterways were highly polluted. Fishing on Lake Erie was banned, and dumped factory waste actually caused the water in the Cuyahoga River near Cleveland, Ohio, to catch on fire. Since the enaction of strict pollution-control laws and the activism of the Environmental Protection Agency (EPA), twice as many lakes and streams are safe for fishing and swimming as were in 1970. Acid rain occurs when chemical pollutants from industrial sources

At one time, America was dotted with huge smokestack factories, symbolizing the country's commitment to heavy industries such as steel, automobiles, and large machinery. These factories used coal or oil to fire their furnaces. The smog that was created polluted much of the country. Air pollution is caused by the particles that are emitted when fuels burn. The residue returns to earth as acid rain, which can be transported over long distances and cause damage to plants, animals, soil, water, and humans. *Library of Congress*

combine with rain or snow to contaminate water sources, plants, and animals. Acid rain levels have been reduced by one-half. The lead-fuel-guzzling, smoke-belching automobiles of the 1940s and 1950s have given way to reengineered vehicles using lead-free gasoline. Because of emission controls built into automobiles since the 1980s, there is today less than 5 percent the pollution produced by the 1970 models.

National air pollution emissions:		
	1970	1994
Particulate matter (in thousands of tons)	13,044	3,705
Lead (in tons)	219,471	4,956

Source: U.S. Bureau of the Census, *Statistical Abstract*

Some credit author Rachel Carson with awakening interest in the ecological dangers that threatened the health and safety of the world. *Silent Spring*, her best-selling book, specifically targeted the dangers of pesticide use and soon became the "bible" of a fast-growing environmental movement. That movement first met with scorn from manufacturers and government officials. Only when people began to understand the effects of ecology on public health did they begin to influence industry and government thinking.

New York State Department of Health / Wadsworth Center

Strict environmental laws began to be enacted during the 1970s. In his State of the Union Address to Congress in 1970, President Richard M. Nixon said, "The great question of the seventies is: Shall we surrender to our surroundings or shall we make our

In the 1950s and 1960s, many rivers, lakes, and streams became unusable because of pollution. The photograph at lower left shows water pollution in Hammond, Indiana. Oil, industrial wastewater, raw sewage, acid rain, and chemical wastes flowed uncontested into America's most pristine waters. Three-fourths of America's rivers were undrinkable and unswimmable. The Clean Water Act of 1972 led to the substantial cleaning up of America's water resources. The main goals of the Act were to make rivers and streams fishable and swimmable and halt the dumping of pollutants. *Library of Congress*

Library of Congress

peace with nature and begin to make reparations for the damage we have done to our air, to our land and to our water?"

The long-ignored concern for the environment resulted in widespread ecological disasters. Coal strip mining in Appalachia contaminated rivers and streams by causing acids, sediments, and metals to drain from the exposed coal beds. Debris from deep-cut mines in mountains, loosened by rain, fell onto farms and homes. Alaska in the late 1970s became a battleground between developers keen to harvest the mineral riches of the forty-ninth state and environmentalists just as keen to preserve the state's unique natural beauty.

Today, we are all aware of the benefits of recycling. Growing numbers of Americans have become accustomed to separating newspapers, cans, bottles, and magazines for recycling. In the 1950s and 1960s, those items were routinely tossed out with the rubbish, adding to growing mountains of trash. It was estimated that in 1960 alone the average American family discarded 750 cans.

For years, the use of asbestos as an insulating and fireproofing material had been widespread in homes, factories, ships, and schools. Although the hazards of asbestos were known in the 1930s, the usefulness of the material was far more important than any health concerns. During World War II and thereafter, asbestos was a key component in shipbuilding and other war industries. It was used without any warnings to the public. Workers who in the 1930s and 1940s contracted asbestosis, a progressive form of lung cancer, nearly always died from breathing the fibers. At least one major tobacco company, Lorillard, was later accused of using filters containing a form of asbestos later banned by most countries in its Kent brand cigarettes of the early 1950s.

Many American homes, long considered a place of refuge and safety, turned out to be sources of cancer-producing agents. "Home, sweet home" was not as safe as everyone thought. Asbestos or formaldehyde in insulation, nitrosamines in the breakfast bacon, and smoke from wood-burning stoves have been linked to cancer. Radon gas from decaying radium gathering in the soil under basements posed yet another cancer threat.

Even home gardens back in the 1950s and 1960s were not as safe as we sometimes imagined. DDT, a powder used originally to disinfect soldiers of body lice during World War II, was used with abandon as a powerful insecticide. Trucks and airplanes sprayed clouds of DDT over fields and homes. Only years later was it revealed that the chemical was a dangerous cancer agent.

Dirty air enveloped large cities across the country and awakened residents to the health consequences of air pollution. In August 1967, the mayor of New York City issued a pollution health alert. "The city has taken preventive steps," he announced. He ordered that automobiles could be used only for business purposes or necessary trips and halted all burning of rubbish at city incinerators. The weather conditions that caused the pollution soon passed but reappeared in succeeding years. Three years later, the mayor had to declare a first-stage pollution alert as New York at the same time suffered from a severe power shortage that affected the use of air conditioners.

Marbeth

During the past twenty years, we have become increasingly concerned about the worldwide state of the environment. Photographs and data from earth-circling satellites have made us aware of such problems as climate change, ozone loss, and deforestation. Satellite technology has also demonstrated to us the interconnectedness of all the world's countries and the need to work cooperatively to solve environmental problems.

During the 1940s and 1950s, Congress debated new environmental regulations as chemical factory wastes continued to seep through the ground and smokestacks belched poisonous fumes into the air. In Pittsfield, Massachusetts, chemical waste from a General Electric plant routinely seeped into the adjacent Housatonic River. The company even trucked soil later found to have been contaminated with PCB, a suspected cancer-causing agent, from its site as fill for homes in the area. As a public service, the company provided free soil to home owners for their lawns and gardens. No one then recognized the health and environmental dangers of PCB.

For decades, a canal in Niagara Falls, New York, was legally used as a dumping site for a chemical company's toxic waste. Between 1942 and 1953, the company dumped over twenty-one tons of chemical waste there. In the 1950s, the dump was closed and capped, and as the area increased in population, a school was built on top of the capped land. Years of construction in the area ultimately disrupted the clay cap and led to the discharge of the chemical wastes into the area's water supply.

The quality of America's water has improved greatly since the 1950s, although problems still exist. Fish now thrive in waters that were once polluted.

From time to time, children came home with skin rashes or chemical burns after playing outside. At other times, residents noticed that areas of vegetation died without apparent reason. Beginning in 1976, the symptoms increased and worsened. Residents were at first mystified, then frightened by foul-smelling liquids bubbling out of the ground. Neighbors also noticed that their area suffered a higher-than-normal rate of birth defects, leukemia, and mental retardation.

After numerous complaints to health authorities, it was revealed that the residents were living on a former waste disposal site. The state health commissioner called the area a "serious threat and danger to the health and safety of those living near it" and recommended that children and pregnant women leave the area at once. Over four hundred chemicals were identified in the canal, some in levels exceeding five thousand times the maximum safe level. Two hundred thirty-six families were uprooted and relocated. But that was only the beginning. The residents of Love Canal suddenly found their modest homes worthless. Who would want to buy a contaminated house? After much debate, the government finally stepped in to buy the homes and relocate the residents.

On August 7, 1978, President Jimmy Carter declared the nation's first nonnatural environmental disaster. The location was the quiet, close-knit community surrounding New York State's Love Canal, near Niagra Falls. From the air, it looked like any other residential area. But beneath the surface were tons of toxic chemical wastes that were rising to the surface and endangering the health of the local residents. The Love Canal experience led to the enactment in 1980 of the Superfund Act to clean up dangerous waste sites nationwide. *New York State Department of Health Photography Unit/Wadsworth Center*

We've made great strides against pollution. Air quality in the United States is better now than it was in 1950. Rivers, once so badly polluted that people were afraid of contracting diseases if they fell in, now support boating, fishing, and swimming. All is not perfect, but thanks to stricter governmental intervention, the condition of the environment has shown great improvement.

Carol Browner, administrator of the EPA, described the advances as follows:

Over the past two decades the implementation of federal laws has contributed to improvements in environmental quality in this country. In virtually every American city, the air is cleaner than it was twenty-five years ago. Water quality in thousands of miles of rivers and streams is much improved. Hundreds of hazardous waste sites are being cleaned up and the use of several especially hazardous chemicals has been restricted or banned entirely.[1]

Traveling by automobile in the 1950s was often a time-consuming and frustrating exercise. Superhighways did not exist, and all traffic flowed on crowded, narrow roads lined with dirty gas stations, "greasy spoon" restaurants, and primitive cabins, forerunners of today's roadside motels. When President Dwight David Eisenhower signed the 1956 National System of Interstate and Defense Highways Act, he literally changed the face of the United States.

For the first time, faster and safer roads linked together all parts of the country. At the height of the Cold War with the Soviet Union, when Americans lived with the

During the mid-1950s, in the neighborhood of Malverne Oaks South, Long Island, a strange and eerie phenomenon would take place at the beginning of each summer. They were hot and sultry days, and I remember one year sitting curbside with my friends Ellen and Barbara, chatting about who would go first in a game, "A, My Name Is Alice." Suddenly, a small red jeep appeared, followed by the blaring sound of a loud horn. As soon as we heard the noise, we all got up and ran to our respective houses like mice fleeing from a pursuing cat. The screams echoed in the neighborhood . . . "Fog Man, Fog Man." Once in the house, I would crawl under the kitchen table and hide scrunched up in a ball, eyes shut, until it was safe to come out. Upon reemerging, I recall looking out the window and seeing a neighborhood engulfed in a whitish cloud . . . thick fog made it impossible to see the house across from us. Within ten minutes the fog dissipated, and we all knew it was safe to venture outside again. A strong smell of pesticide permeated the air, and we knew the "Fog Man" would return.

—Joanne Shorser-Gentile

constant fear of nuclear attack, these roads were built to serve an important defense role. In the event of an enemy attack, military convoys could quickly move throughout the country. These new highways were also designated civil defense evacuation routes in the event of a nuclear attack, permitting families to escape to safety in their own automobiles. (The planners evidently did not anticipate flat tires, auto accidents, and broken-down autos, which could instantly clog any of the highways.)

But enemy attacks were not the only potential source of nuclear radiation danger for Americans. During the 1950s and 1960s, the U.S. government conducted a series of nuclear tests in Nevada. The first American nuclear test was conducted at Alamogordo, New Mexico, in July 1945. Since then, over two thousand separate tests

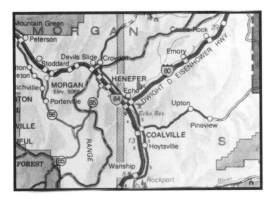

have been conducted by the United States and the handful of other nuclear world powers. Areas surrounding test sites witnessed high rates of birth defects and cancer-related illnesses many attribute to the radioactive clouds that drifted above them after the detonations.

Radioactive fallout from those tests was ingested by people and animals in the air they breathed or the food they ate. Other related problems were radiation sickness, burns, cancer, and various diseases. National security concerns at the time far outweighed any potential health dangers. Arjun Makhijani, president of the Institute for Energy and Environmental Research, said, "They knew when the tests were and chose not to warn the population, and they located the test site in the West, knowing there would be fallout over the whole country."[2]

Known nuclear tests worldwide, 1945-1996:		
Test Type	U.S.Total	World Total
Atmospheric	215	528
Underground	815	1,517
Total	1,030	2, 045

Source: Greenpeace.

During the 1956 presidential election, the Democratic Party candidate Adlai Stevenson spoke out about these tests and claimed that "growing children are the principal potential sufferers." His supporters accused the government of concealing the fact that the nation's milk supply had been contaminated by strontium 90 fallout from the hydrogen bomb explosions. The chairman of the Atomic Energy Commission (AEC) responded, "The facts are directly contrary to the charge."

Only years later did the government finally admit that the earlier atomic bomb blasts affected the health of greater numbers of people than previously imagined. In 1983, President Ronald Reagan ordered a nationwide examination of radiation fallout during the 1950s. The study discovered that all Americans received at least some radiation fallout during that period. People living closest to or directly downwind of the blast sites were heavily exposed. But a study by the National Cancer Institute revealed that radioactive materials also fell on farms as far away as New York State. In turn, the radiation was absorbed by crops, farm ani-

The atomic bomb attack on Japan in 1945 marked the beginning of the nuclear age. *National Archives*

mals, and the earth itself. In 1990 Congress passed the Radiation Exposure Compensation Act specifically to compensate individuals who lived in certain areas of Nevada, Arizona, or Utah and contracted illnesses attributed to the bomb blasts.

In 1997, the NCI released the results of a study that concluded that Americans were exposed to varying levels of radioactive iodine 131 for two months following each of ninety atomic tests conducted in Nevada during the 1950s and 1960s. The radiation extended beyond the immediate test site and was detected as far away as New England and the Northwest. The amount of radiation absorbed depended on each person's age at the time of the tests, where they lived, and what foods they ate or drank, particularly milk. Radioactive iodine accumulates in the thyroid gland, and children are particularly vulnerable. Most children probably received three to seven times the average dose of radiation because they drank more milk than adults. The study's director, Bruce Wachholtz, said, "This is a crucial step in understanding the impact of the nuclear weapons tests on public health."[3]

Ralph Nader was responsible for the passage of major federal laws during the 1960s that improved America's health and safety:

1. National Traffic and Motor Vehicle Safety Act, 1966.
2. Wholesale Meat Act, 1967.
3. National Gas Pipeline Safety Act, 1968.
4. Radiation Control for Health and Safety Act, 1968.
5. Wholesale Poultry Products Act, 1968.

After that there was a proliferation not only of nuclear weapons, but of nuclear power stations as well. Nuclear power plants, once thought of as sources of safe, clean power, have not enjoyed a safe history. There have been a large number of incidents resulting in injury and death. One of the most widely reported accidents occurred at the Three Mile Island nuclear plant in Pennsylvania. The core of the nuclear reactor partially melted, resulting in the release of radioactive gases. Nearly one-quarter of a million people temporarily fled the area. No one died at the site at the time of the meltdown, but a study later estimated that a number of infant deaths in the region eventually resulted from the accident.

Strangely, the government also conducted its own medically oriented radiation experiments on citizens. Many were legitimate medical experiments, such as those by the AEC on the use of radioisotopes to diagnose or cure disease. These pioneering experiments led to major advances in nuclear medicine that today save thousands of lives yearly.

Some of those early experiments were conducted in less than ethical (or legal) ways, sometimes without regard for the rights and safety of participants. During the 1940s and 1950s, scientists conducted such an experiment on nineteen retarded boys at the Fernald State School in Massachusetts. The boys, who later recounted that they were selected as members of a special "science club," were fed radioactive milk in an effort to learn more about the human digestive system. None seemed to suffer harmful effects.

Between 1949 and 1969, the United States Army released bacteria and chemical agents in major American cities including New York, San Francisco, and Washington, D.C., to simulate chemical and biological warfare. A number of residents of those cities later reported unexplainable illnesses and birth-related problems. Although the government denied that its practices led to those medical problems, experts agreed that the experiments should have been more carefully conducted.

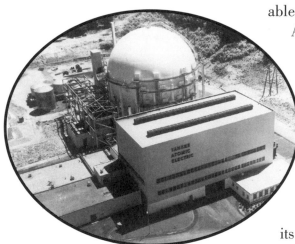

The AEC also conducted radiation experiments in less than ethical ways. In one experiment, scientists injected "persons with a relatively short life expectancy" with plutonium to study its effects on human bodies. In another,

The first nuclear power plant in the United States was opened in 1957 in Shippingport, Pennsylvania. Nuclear power was cheaper to produce than traditional fossil-fuel methods and with proper control did not introduce harmful waste by-products into the atmosphere. Unfortunately, the used fuel of a nuclear power plant is radioactive, and disposing of it has become a major environmental and health concern. Concern for the safety of nuclear reactors in the United States increased after a serious accident at the Three Mile Island nuclear power plant in Pennsylvania. Scientists were able to prevent the escape of radioactive gases into the atmosphere, but it was a close call. The release of radioactive isotopes into the air, such as occurred at the Chernobyl plant in Russia in 1986, can lead to widespread increases in cancer-related deaths and illnesses. Because of these safety issues and increased competition in the electricity business, many nuclear plants are being phased out. The Yankee Rowe plant in Massachusetts is one of many American nuclear power plants to close. *National Archives*

brain-tumor patients were injected with massive amounts of uranium to see how much was needed to induce kidney damage.

Dangers to the public from nuclear radiation continues, but imminent danger from nuclear war has greatly decreased. The end of the Cold War has also ended the nuclear arms race. According to James B. Steinberg, the deputy assistant to President Bill Clinton for national security affairs, there are now "unprecedented opportunities for nuclear arms control."[4] The Comprehensive Test Ban Treaty was signed by President Clinton in 1996 to halt the testing of nuclear weapons. A separate Chemical Weapons Convention went into effect in 1997. Unfortunately, in 1998 both India and Pakistan tested nuclear weapons.

④ Home, Sweet Home

Did television correctly depict the typical 1950s American family? If you watch reruns or videos of any of the popular shows of that era, you might get a definite but skewed view of family life back then. *Ozzie and Harriet* and *Father Knows Best* were two popular shows. They portrayed the petty problems of white families, each composed of a working father, a stay-at-home mother, and assorted well-adjusted children. Unseen by viewers were conditions no one talked about: poverty, discrimination, and the status of women.

"Television permits people who haven't anything to do to watch people who can't do anything."
—Fred Allen, comedian

At first, television was thought to bring families together. At a time when there was just a single set in most homes and only two or three channels to choose from, the entire family would gather in front of the television set just as they had a few years earlier in front of the family radio.
Library of Congress

The idealized family that real families watched on television did have at least one positive influence: It set a national standard for the ways in which families were "supposed" to live and act. The 1950s were a time of change for Americans. In the era following World War II, traditional family life was directly affected by the newly evolving world of work. A rising "middle class" lifted the standard of living but often required the family "breadwinner"—usually the father—to be away from home on business for extended periods of time.

Changes in American Homes:

	1970	1990
New homes with central air-conditioning	34%	76%
Households with cable TV	4 million	55 million
Households with VCRs	0	67 million
Homes without a telephone	13%	5.2%
Homes with microwave ovens	1%	78.8%
Americans finishing high school	51.9%	77.7%
Americans finishing college	13.5%	24.4%
Annual paid vacation days	15.5 days	22.5 days

Source: Federal Reserve Bank of Dallas, 1994.

A result was the availability of extra money for luxury goods. Between 1970 and 1990, the money spent on jewelry and watches doubled, and the number of overseas trips nearly tripled. Today, we all enjoy a higher standard of living thanks to inventions that did not exist twenty years earlier. We watch movies at home on our videocassette recorders; we listen to our favorite musicians performing with the utmost clarity thanks to digital CD technology; we send faxes around the world with the ease of a telephone call; and we exercise at home on fitness equipment available only in gyms twenty years ago and then warm up day-old pepperoni pizza in a microwave oven.

In 1965, only 28 percent of blacks and 69 percent of whites were satisfied with household income. By 1997, satisfaction increased to 53 percent of blacks and 72 percent of whites.

—The Gallup Organization

But no matter how many times June Cleaver, the smiling mother on *Leave It to Beaver*, baked another cake while wearing a pearl necklace, many real mothers led less than ideal lives. Although home life in the 1950s and 1960s was more stable

Television became the center of attraction for many. This cartoon poked fun at the role television had created for itself in family activities. Here a family is depicted at Thanksgiving dinner where everyone is intently watching a football game. *Cover drawing by Alajalov © 1949, The New Yorker Magazine.*

than today, there were disturbing reasons for that outward tranquility. In many states, women were still legally prohibited from serving on juries, signing binding contracts, or having their own credit cards. It was an age when anyone—man, woman, or child—who tried to counter the prevailing status quo was ignored or ridiculed. That was the price to be paid for nonconformity.

A high school home-economics text-book from the 1950s taught girls to assume their roles as dutiful wives:

Have dinner ready. Plan ahead . . . to have a delicious meal on time. This is the best way of letting him know that you have been thinking of him. Your husband should feel he has reached a haven of rest and order. Prepare the children. Comb their hair and, if necessary, change their clothes. They are little treasures and he would like to see them playing the part.[1]

When I was a boy, the *Ed Sullivan Show* was on every Sunday evening. My entire family watched it. One Sunday, February 9, 1964, some friends came over for my eighth birthday. We went downstairs to the big black-and-white TV because several of the girls were excited about watching the show. They said some group called the Beatles was going to be on. Ed introduced them: "Ladies and gentlemen . . . the Beatles." The crowd in the audience and the crowd in my house were screaming. As the show started, I watched in wonder at who these guys were and at the very animated, and I thought weird, reactions by the girls. I soon came to love the "lads" and do to this day.

—Mark Jacobson

Today's husbands and fathers are much more involved in household duties than in the era following World War II. A 1997 Gallup poll concluded that 85 percent of husbands help with housework, 73 percent with cooking, and 57 percent with dishes. (The 1949 figures were, respectively, 62, 40, and 31 percent.)

From newspapers, magazines, and television talk shows, we sometimes get the impression that family life in America has been destroyed by a high divorce rate, working mothers, and money problems. Although most Americans feel it is more difficult to raise a child today, a majority told interviewers for the Gallup poll that they spend more time with their children than their parents spent with them. Also surprising is the fact that while today's families are being pulled apart by their constant activities, over 70 percent of families with children say their family eats dinner together at least five out of seven days a

"[Television] can teach, it can illuminate: yes, and it can even inspire. But it can do so only to the extent that humans are determined [to pursue] it to those ends. Otherwise, it is merely wires and lights in a box. There is a great and perhaps decisive battle to be fought against ignorance, intolerance, and indifference. This weapon of television could be useful."
—Edward R. Murrow, newscaster, 1958

Elvis Presley changed the beat of America and the world. Rock and Roll music, when it began the climb to popularity in the 1950s, was thought to corrupt the morals of young people. Elvis did nothing to make it more respectable, but he did make it popular. Parents recoiled as their sons tried to imitate Elvis's walk, image, and tough stage manner. The boys dressed in black leather jackets and "ducktail" haircuts while girls screamed and swooned at Elvis concerts. *National Archives*

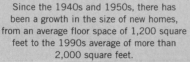

Since the 1940s and 1950s, there has been a growth in the size of new homes, from an average floor space of 1,200 square feet to the 1990s average of more than 2,000 square feet.

Armstrong World Industries

week, with over one-third indicating that their family eats dinner together all seven days. Furthermore, extended family members such as relatives and friends have become a support network providing many children with additional feelings of security.

Television in the 1950s and 1960s portrayed an image of America that was white and middle class. African Americans and other American minorities were shown as stereotypes in the situation comedies and dramas Americans watched during those years.

American homes have changed greatly over the past fifty years. Since World War II, there have been dramatic changes in the size, design, and construction of the typical American house. The average new

Every American city had its poor areas with substandard, crowded, and unhealthy living conditions. This section of New York City was typical of just such a neighborhood. It shows tenements on LaSalle Street before being demolished for construction of the General Grant Housing Project. In the late 1960s, in response to the activist leadership of President Lyndon B. Johnson, a cabinet-level Department of Housing and Urban Development was created to assure adequate housing for the neediest Americans. Soon, neighborhoods such as this were torn down and replaced with high-rise housing projects. The good news was that the apartments offered clean, healthy living conditions. The bad news was that because so many people with social and economic problems crowded into small areas, some projects became the breeding ground for crime and drugs. By the mid-1990s, some of the most notorious of these projects were torn down and replaced by less dense, low-rise apartments. *National Archives*

Percentage of families living below the poverty level:	
1959	1995
18.5%	10.8%

Source: U.S. Bureau of the Census, *Statistical Abstract*

home today has more bathrooms, a bigger kitchen, and greater facility for new technology. Telephone jacks are routinely placed in every room to accommodate telecommuters. Back in the 1950s, one telephone typically served an entire household. Homes began to contain family rooms or dens to provide for the increased leisure time of the American family. If a new house had a garage, it tended to be small and capable of storing one automobile.

Into the mid-1950s, many American houses still did not have central heat. Few had clothes dryers, dishwashers, or air conditioners. The great building boom of that period brought changes. By 1959, 98 percent of all homes had a refrigerator, 77 percent had one television, 73 percent had a washing machine, but only 13 percent had air-conditioning. Into the 1960s, the pleasures of air-conditioning were enjoyed mainly in movie theaters (to draw patrons away from their home television sets) and large department stores. Once air-conditioning became widespread, the face of America was forever changed. In the South especially, where residents used to emerge from their hot houses to sit on front porches and greet neighbors, air-conditioning moved people back into the cool but isolated comfort of their homes.

The growth of the suburbs has changed the image of America.

After World War II, returning veterans needed decent and affordable housing. The growth of suburban housing developments resulted in "look alike" communities, sameness in construction, and populations that were similar in income, educational level, and race. As more people moved to the suburbs, the economy and social interaction between different races was disrupted in many inner cities. *National Archives*

The pioneer in surburban building was William Levitt. Levittown, on Long Island, New York, was the first of his major housing communities. Between 1947 and 1951, Levitt built more than 17,000 houses in former potato fields. His planned community consisted of parks, shopping centers, playgrounds, swimming pools, and bowling alleys. Throughout the country, other builders followed Levitt's plan. The era of American suburban life began. The results were not all positive.

In once-vibrant cities, millions of residents—who could afford to—moved out. The middle class of working, young, professional families abandoned the cities to the very rich and the poor. Because the moves generally involved a shift of less than thirty miles, the family breadwinner had to commute back to the city for work. When people reflect on their happy suburban lives in the 1950s and 1960s, where everyone seemed to share similar lifestyles and economic status, they tend to ignore what was lacking: diversity. There was a sameness about life in the suburbs that did not exist in the cities they left behind. Gone was the variety of people, cultures, and buildings that made for vibrant experiences. Because there were no government restrictions on discrimination, many housing developments like Levittown had regulations to prohibit sales to African Americans and other minorities.

The mid-1960s was the era of President Lyndon B. Johnson's "Great Society." The program had many successes that benefited disadvantaged people. Prior to the federal government takeover of welfare programs, benefits to poor people varied from

> *Was that two rings or three?*
> Whenever the telephone rang in our house in the 1950s, we had to listen carefully to the number of rings. We had a "party line." Four other households shared the same number. The only difference was that each household had a letter designation at the end of the telephone number. Our number was Chelsea 3-4861J. Another house's number would have ended in an "R" or another letter. You were only supposed to pick up the phone on your ring. Many times, when you couldn't tell how many rings there were, people in the different homes would pick up their phones at the same time and say, "Hello." The usual response was, "Get off the line. This is my call!"
> —Norman Finkelstein

From the moment Thomas Edison introduced the benefits of electricity, Americans have been looking for ways to make everyday chores easier. Electric toasters and vacuum cleaners became popular beginning in the 1920s, but not every family could afford them. By the 1950s, these and other devices had been improved, streamlined, and made more affordable. In the years after World War II, as Americans began earning more money, advertising enticed consumers to part with their money to enjoy the benefits of timesaving appliances. With the woman's role as the primary housekeeper, much of the advertising was targeted at them. *The Hoover Company*

state to state. The results were often unfair and embarrassing to people in poverty. The poor were often treated as common criminals and given little sense of dignity. The overseeing of welfare programs by the federal government ensured a minimum level of benefits. A major success of the Great Society legislation was the Medicare program for elderly citizens. Medicare guaranteed them a level of quality health care that did not previously exist.

Among the failures were well-intentioned attempts to provide decent housing for the poor of America's inner cities. Old tenement buildings gave way to large concrete apartment buildings. These high-rise "projects" became confined spawning grounds for crime. Their size and mazelike, sterile designs led to social breakdown and juvenile delinquency. "Throw them together and they will form a community," the planners in the 1950s wrongly thought. In the 1990s, many of these buildings were torn down and their residents moved to better-designed housing.

In 1963, 45 percent of blacks and 82 percent of whites were satisfied with their standard of living. In 1997, 74 percent of blacks and 87 percent of whites were satisfied.

—The Gallup Organization

Suburban houses were built for comfort and provided a special refuge for women, most of whom remained home while their husbands went off to work. The emphasis for women was on marriage, children, and family life. Many people preferred to stay in a bad marriage than suffer the stigma of divorce. In the 1950s, the average divorce rate was less than half of what it became in the 1990s.

The male-to-female ratio of employment:		
	Male	Female
1950	72%	28%
1960	68%	32%
1970	63%	37%
1980	58%	42%
1990	57%	43%

But as appealing as the Ozzie-and-Harriet lifestyle may appear, it was not totally fulfilling. Unhappy housewives, trapped by a limiting lifestyle, whiled away their afternoons watching mindless television game shows and soap operas. A growing number of women turned to alcohol for escape or became dependent on the newly emerging brands of prescription tranquilizers. Sales of tranquilizers reached $5 million between 1954, when they first became available, and 1959. *The New York Times* reported on a medical and psychological study of one suburban community: "Life in growing suburbia, specifically in Englewood, New Jersey, is giving people ulcers, heart attacks and other 'tension-related psychosomatic disorders.'"[1] The researchers found that "everything from crab grass to high taxes played a role in emotional difficulties." Today, men and women find it easier to divorce. In spite of the serious difficulties divorce brings to families, it permits individuals a way out of oppressive or abusive marriages.

Today, nearly half of all medical students in the United States are women. That figure is truly amazing considering the fact the most medical schools in this country did not actively admit women until the mid-1960s! In 1963, Dr. Nina Braunwald was the only female heart surgeon in the United States. She is pictured here holding a test chamber containing an artificial heart valve she helped develop. *National Archives*

By 1960, conditions had changed. Twice as many women held jobs outside the home as had in 1940. "All we're asking," said Addie Wyatt, a union leader, "is that we be recognized as full partners—at home, at work, in the world at large."[2] At first, the types of jobs women held offered no competition to men. Women tended to be clerical workers or salespeople, conceding "the top rungs to men."[3] As women took on more important and more time-consuming jobs outside the home, changes had to be made. Married couples made new arrangements to share routine household chores.

Author Emily Kimbrough wrote, "Consider . . . the persistence of the qualifying phrase . . . 'remarkable for a woman.' Why should it be remarkable that a woman can be successful in business? It seems to me far more remarkable that she is so seldom in the top position."[4]

Frances Perkins, Secretary of Labor from 1933-1945, was the first woman Cabinet member. *Mount Holyoke College Archives and Special Collections*

Women in public life were a rarity at midcentury. Prior to the mid-1970s, only two women, Frances Perkins and Oveta Culp Hobby, had ever served in a president's cabinet. No woman had ever been elected governor of a state. None had ever served as chief justice of a state supreme court. None had been managing editor of a major U.S. newspaper. But 1975 saw Carla Hills become secretary of the Department of Housing and Urban Development. Ella Grasso was elected governor of Connecticut. Susie Sharp became the chief justice of the North Carolina Supreme Court, and Carol Sutton was appointed managing editor of the *Louisville Courier-Journal*.

Today, more women attend and graduate from college and graduate school than in the past. In fact, men and women earn their degrees in equal proportions. What is most exciting is that women are finding new satisfaction in their jobs by making their way into professions that were previously limited to men. Gradually, women have overcome generations of discriminatory traditions. But it is still not easy. "I work twice as hard as a man," one female executive said, "just to prove that I am not a dumb woman."[5]

⑤ We Never Locked Our Doors

If all you did was watch television, you might get the mistaken idea that crime and violence are today's number-one industries. News stories from around the world highlight wars, bombings, and continued ethnic strife. Horrible crimes head the local and national news. For recreation, drama and adventure programs entertain us with graphic stories of crime and violence. With all the fear that surrounds us, wouldn't it be great to return to the eras of our parents and grandparents? There was less violence, less fear back then. Right?

The Cold War pitted two nuclear superpowers against each other. In 1958, Soviet Premier Nikita Khrushchev attempted to force the United States and its allies to relinquish control over West Berlin. The West held fast and refused to bargain with the Soviet Union. That crisis passed but resurfaced in 1961. In August 1961, Khrushchev, under pressure from East German leaders to stem the flow of its citizens to the freedom of the West, ordered the building of the Berlin Wall. Fearful that American rights to West Berlin were in jeopardy again, President John F. Kennedy ordered armed United States troops and armored trucks to travel through East German territory to West Berlin. The result was a tense confrontation at Checkpoint Charlie, a crossing point from the American sector into East Berlin. Neither side was willing to risk a wider confrontation and each warily backed off. The danger was temporarily defused. *National Archives*

Despite wartime censorship and controlled news, World War II entered the living rooms of America through radio broadcasts and newspaper reports. In movie theaters, people of all ages watched newsreels of actual fighting, then sat back for a main feature film that often con-tained realistically contrived scenes of combat. When the war ended in 1945, the deeply felt fears did not disappear. In place of heated combat with Japanese and German armies, the United States entered into a prolonged cold war with the Soviet Union and its communist philosophy of world revolution.

Anxiety and disbelief gripped America. The red flags of commu-nism seemed to flutter across the globe with one communist victory after another. In 1949, Communist revolutionaries in China success-fully overthrew the existing gov-ernment after a three-year civil war. That same year, the Soviet Union jolted the world by testing an atomic bomb, thereby joining the United States as a world nuclear power. How could the Soviets have attained such scientific knowledge so quickly after the devastation they suffered during World War II? How did they so quickly become a nuclear power and deprive the United States of its role as the world's sole superpower?

Berlin, Germany, was the center of Cold War attention during the 1950s and 1960s. Following World War II, Germany was divided into four zones, which were later formed into two separate countries—West Germany, friendly to the West, and East Germany, which became part of the Soviet bloc. The capital city, Berlin, totally surrounded by the Soviets, was itself divided into zones. West Berlin symbolized democracy and free-dom; East Berlin was communist. There was never any doubt which form of govern-ment the majority of Germans preferred. Between 1945 and 1961 over three million East Germans "voted with their feet" and escaped into West Germany, many by way of West Berlin. At the height of the Cold War, the communists decided to build a wall to keep their residents from fleeing. East German workers near the Brandenburg Gate reinforced the wall under the watchful eye of communist police. The Wall stood in place as a "wall of shame" until 1989 when communism fell and the two Germanies were united. *National Archives*

> "No superdeep shelter can save them from an all-shattering blow from this weapon."
> —Soviet Premier Nikita Khrushchev, in a nuclear threat to the United States, 1961

Many thought the Soviet Union could only have achieved such advances with help from

American traitors. Across America, anticommunist feelings exploded into paranoid fear of the Soviet Union and communism. Politicians used irrational fear to paint their opponents as "Reds" or "pinkos." In 1950, the Internal Security Act instituted regulations for rooting out Communists and their sympathizers from government. Live televised congressional hearings focused on alleged Communists and workers in major industries and government agencies thought to be communist sympathizers.

America in the 1950s was a land in near panic. The fear was dramatically heightened by the outbreak of the Korean War in 1950 and expectations of imminent Soviet nuclear attacks on American cities. Some citizens built bomb shelters in their homes, while government officials designated evacuation routes from major cities and staged civil-defense drills in schools. In the White House basement, an air-raid shelter with nine-foot-thick steel and concrete walls was outfitted with an elaborate radio and telephone system to keep President Truman in contact with the government in the event of an enemy air attack. Students were trained to "duck and cover" in their classrooms, while mock air-raid drills on the streets kept their parents alert. Everyone was more than familiar with the piercing shrill of air-raid sirens. At home, some families who could afford the cost built well-equipped but useless underground fallout shelters. They wanted to believe that if America were annihilated by a massive nuclear attack, they could survive intact with the help of canned soups and four gallons of drinking water. It was difficult for people to understand that even if they survived the initial attack and massive doses of lethal radiation, it could be years before the outside air would be safe to breathe again.

Americans were treated to an increasing number of "anti-Red" films at their local movie houses. Titles such as *I Was a Communist for the F.B.I.*, *I Married a Communist*, and *The Red Menace* helped fuel anticommunism. Bubble gum trading cards taught children to "fight the Commies." Traitors lurked everywhere; at least, that's what most people thought. Students continuously faced the fearful realities of the time as the world lurched from one heart-stopping event to another: the Korean War, the Bay of Pigs invasion of Cuba, the construction of the Berlin Wall, and the Cuban missile crisis. In school, teachers taught students to get under desks and tables at the first warning flash of a nuclear attack. On the streets, there were signs pointing to the civil defense escape routes out of cities. At home, radio and television programs continuously portrayed the evil consequences of the "Red Menace." Automobile radios came from the factory with "Conelrad" frequency markings. Listeners were to tune in to this frequency for instructions in the event of a nuclear attack.

It was the era of McCarthyism. Joseph R. McCarthy was the Republican junior U.S. senator from the state of Wisconsin. In the early 1950s, he became the most widely known—and the most feared—member of the U.S. Senate. He was the country's best-known anticommunist spokesperson. McCarthy tried to ban books he claimed were written by Communists or pinko sympathizers. His list included some of America's most talented writers and most important literary works. Again and again he repeated his famous words, "I have here in my hand . . ." and went on to

1952—I felt very proud of the "dog tag" that hung around my neck. Dog tags were for soldiers. They wore them for identification purposes in case they were killed or injured. The information embossed on the tags would identify who they were, what military outfit they belonged to, and their blood type. I was in the fifth grade and had no intention at that time of joining the army. Each student in my school was issued a dog tag on a link chain to wear. The tag was imprinted with my name, address, date of birth, and religion. In case of a nuclear attack, my body could be easily identified—that is, if the dog tag survived and there were others still alive to receive the information. It all seemed very strange at the time and even stranger today.

—Norman Finkelstein

make yet another unsubstantiated charge and to destroy yet another innocent person's reputation. Otherwise innocent individuals were dismissed from jobs, "blacklists" of suspected "disloyal" people were circulated widely, and an unwritten state of "self-censorship" enveloped the nation.

"I will not get into the gutter with that guy."
—President Dwight D. Eisenhower, speaking about Senator Joseph McCarthy

People stopped visiting friends who were under suspicion. They feared that government investigators might be copying down and reporting license numbers. A *New York Times* article in 1951 told the story of 110 scholars, "among them some of the illustrious minds in our generation," who lost their jobs at the University of California because they refused to take a loyalty oath.[1] The search for Communists and traitors was relentless.

People simply suspected of liberal views lost their jobs or were blacklisted from other positions. When well-known film writers and directors refused to testify and inform on colleagues before the House Un-American Activities Committee, they were blacklisted. The so-called Hollywood Ten found themselves unable to find jobs in the film industry for decades. Many Americans tragically discovered that rights granted them under the Constitution of the United States could not protect them from the self-righteous, rabid "Commie" hunters to whom a false accusation or malicious rumor was a sign of certain guilt. "Better Dead Than Red" was the motto of those times.

In the early 1950s, Joseph McCarthy was the most feared member of the United States Senate. Taking advantage of the strong anti-communist feeling of the era, he shamelessly and shrilly scattered accusations of communism and disloyalty against prominent Americans. His hearings on alleged communist infiltration of the army were broadcast live. *George Tames/NYT Permissions*

Many children of those blacklisted individuals could not escape the fear and anxiety of their parents. Casey Murrow, son of the famous news broadcaster Edward R. Murrow, revealed that his father often helped blacklisted writers and journalists. "There were a lot of threats," Casey later said, "against them [his parents] and against me. I never knew what was going on at the time. They worked so hard to keep things normal." Once during the McCarthy era, Murrow told his wife, "We must never allow Casey to be unattended." For a long time thereafter, Casey was escorted daily by his mother or a maid to and from school. One of Ed's colleagues recalled, "Ed always felt there were times during the McCarthy period when his phone was bugged."[2]

U.S. confidence fell apart in 1957 when the Soviet Union launched *Sputnik*, the first artificial satellite to circle the earth. This milestone cast fear throughout the country that our way of life might be doomed. Foreign headlines screamed, RUSSIA WINS SPACE RACE and RUSSIA LAUNCHES A MOON. President Eisenhower tried to put the event in focus

Legends exist about the "flower children" of the 1960s, the hippies. Dissatisfied with traditional political and social life, these young people emphasized a communal life which often included the use of illegal drugs and counterculture music. While all young people in the country did not adopt this lifestyle, aspects of this "dropout" life affected a growing number of young Americans. © *Lisa Law*

at a news conference: "As far as the satellite itself is concerned, that does not raise my apprehensions, not one iota."[3] But the Cold War continued to be fought in the United Nations, in propaganda, in threatening scenes at the Berlin Wall, and in the Cuban missile crisis. From October 15–28, 1962, the world teetered on the brink of nuclear disaster. The Soviet Union had secretly shipped offensive missiles to Cuba, just ninety miles away from the United States. Nikita Khrushchev, the Soviet prime minister, threatened that he would "bury" the United States. In the end, it was the Soviet Union that collapsed. After 1991, the United States remained the world's only and uncontested superpower.

The Vietnam War created another form of tension within the United States, as it pitted protesting students against supporters of the war. It was one of the few times in

Library of Congress

world history when so many students militantly attempted to alter the decisions of a government. At 2:30 A.M. on May 10, 1968, one thousand New York City police officers, armed with warrants signed by the trustees of Columbia University, marched onto the campus to begin evicting hundreds of demonstrating students who had seized control of a university building. Universities, which until then were considered quiet places of intellectual curiosity, had become, in the tumultuous era of the 1960s, centers of political activism. It was the age of the "hippies," illegal drugs, and "flower power," a symbol of peace.

Events at Kent State University on May 4, 1970, dramatically changed the way Americans viewed the protests against the Vietnam War. An escalating series of protests and demonstrations resulted in the stationing of Ohio National Guard troops on the campus. The student demands were no different from those on other campuses: an end to the Vietnam War, the removal of the National Guard, and the cessation of the school's Reserve Officers' Training Corps program (ROTC), which trained future military officers. By noon, several hundred students had gathered around the campus Victory Bell as one thousand more watched from a nearby hillside.

> "I don't think we've got much time on these missiles."
> —President John F. Kennedy, on the Cuban missile crisis, 1962

The peaceful demonstration was disrupted by a National Guard officer with a bullhorn. "This is an order," the officer said. "Leave this area immediately. This is an order. Disperse!" The order was greeted by obscenities and jeering from the assembled students. When several rocks were thrown from the crowd toward a passing army jeep, guard troops were ordered to fire tear gas canisters. Students threw additional rocks at the troops, and the troops fired more tear gas. The escalating confrontation ended when, under questionable circumstances, members of the National Guard fired live ammunition at the students. Four students were killed and nine wounded. Some of those shot were bystanders who were not actively involved in the demonstration. No one was able to ascertain who fired the first shot or who issued an order to fire. The shooting of unarmed American students shocked the country.

Racial violence and discrimination were factors of life in the 1940s and 1950s. Even a shortage in nursing personnel in the early 1950s could not put African American nurses into white hospitals. "Why," asked Thurgood Marshall, who would later become a member of the Supreme Court, "of all the multitudinous groups of people in this country do

Dr. Martin Luther King Jr. was the conscience of the civil rights movement. King was born in Atlanta, Georgia, and was educated at Morehouse College, Crozier Seminary and received his doctorate in theology from Boston University. Dr. King preached a doctrine of nonviolence. He inspired black and white Americans to actively fight segregation. "We're through with tokenism," Dr. King said, "We're through with we've-done-more-for-your-people-than-anyone-else-ism. We can't wait any longer. Now is the time." White and black clergy, students, and others dedicated to ending segregation headed South to participate in sit-ins, pray-ins, buy-ins, freedom rides, and freedom marches. *Ratner Center for the Study of Conservative Judaism, The Jewish Theological Seminary of America*

Thurgood Marshall was the first African American member of the United States Supreme Court. He was appointed in 1967 by President Lyndon B. Johnson. For years, as an attorney and later as head of the NAACP Legal Defense Fund, Marshall was at the forefront of the landmark civil rights court cases of the century. In 1956 he represented Ms. Autherine Lucy who was seeking admission to the segregated University of Alabama. "Maybe you can't override prejudice overnight," Marshall said, "but the Emancipation Proclamation was issued in 1863, ninety odd years ago. I believe in gradualism and I also believe that ninety odd years is pretty gradual." *NAACP Legal Defense and Educational Fund*

"Ending segregation would mark the beginning of the end of civilization in the South as we have known it," declared Governor James Byrnes of South Carolina. Confrontations between local authorities and federal officials quickly escalated. National Guard soldiers were often called in to maintain order. When President Eisenhower ordered federal troops to Little Rock, Arkansas, in 1957 to force the desegregation of the high school, he said, "Mob rule cannot be allowed to override the decision of our courts." Southern resistance continued into the 1960s. At his 1963 inauguration, Governor George Wallace of Alabama thundered, "I draw the line in the dust and toss the gauntlet before the feet of tyranny, and I say segregation now, segregation tomorrow, segregation forever!" *Middleton A. "Spike" Harris Collection, Schomburg Center for Research in Black Culture, New York Public Library*

Civil rights demonstrations were not limited to the South. In the North, stores were picketed during the 1960s to protest segregated policies of Southern stores. *Archives of Labor and Urban Affairs, Wayne State University*

you have to single out Negroes and give them this special treatment?"[4]

In 1896, the Supreme Court ruled in *Plessy v. Ferguson* in an 8-to-1 decision that segregation by race did not mean racial discrimination. "Separate but equal" became a way of life in America until 1954. It was overturned because in practice it completely and unequally segregated the races.

Rosa Parks was tired. After a hard day's work, she boarded a city bus in Montgomery, Alabama, in 1955. Local law dictated that whites and blacks were to be separated, not only at drinking fountains, restaurants, schools, hospitals, and parks, but also on buses. Blacks sat in the rear, whites in the front. Ms. Parks sat down in an available seat and removed her tight shoes. A few stops later, a white man boarded the crowded bus. There was standing room only, and the man demanded the seat from Rosa Parks. Politely, she answered, "No, I'm sorry." She was arrested and taken to jail. For one year, the African American residents of

Montgomery boycotted the city's bus system. The protest was led by a young minister who soon became world famous, Dr. Martin Luther King Jr.

For a year, until the Supreme Court ruled that segregation of buses was illegal, the African American residents of Montgomery boycotted the city bus system. While they peacefully walked or arranged for private transportation, the city buses were barely used and the company suffered economically. The newly arrived minister at the Dexter Avenue Baptist Church, Dr. Martin Luther King Jr., was asked to lead the boycott. *National Archives*

America watched the civil rights struggle unfold on their television screens. Nonviolent protest, inspired by Dr. King, led to picketing, "sit-ins," "freedom rides," and peaceful demonstrations that were often disrupted by violence from segregationists. Bombings of African American homes and churches escalated. Innocent men, women, and children were injured or killed. African American students were denied admission to state universities in the South as well as integrated public schools. When Autherine Lucy was finally admitted to the University of Alabama in 1956, riots erupted and she was expelled. Her first day at the university, she later said, was "a day I'll never want to live through again."[5]

In 1957, President Eisenhower ordered federal troops into Little Rock, Arkansas, to protect the rights of African American students trying to integrate Little Rock High School. The nation was shocked by the sight of armed troops leading black students past jeering crowds of whites. Forty years later, President Clinton recalled the event that "seared the heart and stirred the conscience of our nation. . . . A fifteen-year-old girl wearing a crisp black and white dress, carrying only a notebook, surrounded by large crowds of boys and girls, men and women, soldiers and police officers, her head held high, her eyes fixed straight ahead. And she is utterly alone."[6]

As the wall of segregation slowly crumbled, the nation witnessed a continuous flow of violence. In 1961, a group of black and white freedom riders testing the federal rule that outlawed segregation in interstate travel journeyed south by bus. Just outside Anniston, Alabama, the bus was pursued by carloads of local white toughs. The bus veered into a ditch and came to a stop. Rocks smashed the windows, and a firebomb was thrown inside. The riders tumbled out to escape the inferno and were met with the blows of fists and clubs. Police reacted with indifference. A few days later, riders on another bus arrived in Montgomery, Alabama, where they were beaten with pipes and chains. Seeking refuge in a black church, they were saved from the fury of an angry white mob by the timely arrival of armed U.S. marshals, hastily organized and sent by President John F. Kennedy.

The nonviolent attitude of most civil rights demonstrators in the South was often met with violent reaction from white mobs and local police. Newspaper photographs showed the uncontrolled use of police dogs, fire hoses, and electric cattle prods by police against peacefully demonstrating men, women, and children. *Schomburg Center for Research in Black Culture, The New York Public Library*

Television brought the reality of racial violence into American homes. On June 21, 1964, three "Freedom Summer" workers disappeared on a drive to Philadelphia, Mississippi, where they had planned to help African Americans register to vote. After an intensive FBI search, the brutally beaten bodies of Andrew Goodman, Michael Schwerner, and James Chaney were found buried in an earthen dam. The violence shocked the nation, but the struggle for civil rights continued. While there is still much work to be done, the United States has witnessed marked improvements in race relations since the 1960s.

Elsewhere in the country, violence grew as economic conditions in cities declined. Middle-class families had moved to the suburbs, leaving the very rich and the very poor behind. Nearly one-quarter of the American population in the 1950s lived below the poverty level. Two million migrant workers toiled under inhumane conditions for meager wages. Those conditions and other factors led to an overall crime rate that was higher than that of the 1990s.

In the mid-1960s, parts of certain American cities were turned into armed camps as decades of frustration erupted in violence. Watts, a section of Los Angeles inhabited mainly by African Americans, was the site of particularly destructive rioting, which escalated over several days. Dozens of people were injured by beatings and shootings. Looting and firebombing destroyed hundreds of businesses. The riots extended to other cities across the nation.

The street violence of the 1960s was preceded by the organized crime activities of the 1950s. Then, the escapades of American gangsters captivated the country. Much of organized crime was highly structured and governed. Known as "the Mob" or "the Mafia," its members controlled gambling, trucking, and labor union activities in America's largest cities. Senator Estes Kefauver of Tennessee was chairman of the U.S. Senate's Special Committee to Investigate Organized Crime in Interstate Commerce. By mid-1951, the voices

In 1961 a group of young people, trained in nonviolence, boarded buses in Washington, DC, and headed for New Orleans, Louisiana. They were testing state and local compliance with a 1960 Supreme Court ruling that legally ended segregation in interstate travel. Outside of Anniston, Alabama, a Greyhound bus was firebombed. As the "Freedom Riders" stumbled from the burning bus, they were met with blows from the fists and clubs of an angry white mob. The riders were severely beaten and many of them lay unconscious and bloody on the ground. *Schomburg Center for Research in Black Culture, The New York Public Library*

and faces of America's legendary gangsters had become familiar to most Americans. Live television brought hearings of the Kefauver committee into homes around the country. Mob chiefs such as Frank Costello and Meyer Lansky dodged and weaved through the questioning of the earnest senators. America discovered the Mafia.

"The two great enemies within our ranks," one senator declared, "the criminals and the communists, often work hand in hand. Wake up America!" Children listened with rapt attention to radio adventure serials in which brave crime fighters did noble battle with criminals, spies, and a wide variety of evil geniuses. If the broadcasts were not enough to frighten young listeners, comic books continued the tension. But nothing compared with the continuing stream of gangster killings and Mob war stories in the daily newspapers and radio and television news programs.

"Mr. Lansky, you're very famous."
—Senator Estes Kefauver to gangster Meyer Lansky, 1951

If gangster stories kept Americans alert and enthralled, the reality of growing street gangs in America's cities kept them frightened. The violent exploits of youth gangs and young motorcycle club members were reported in newspapers and magazines. Such 1950s movies as *The Wild One* vividly revealed an underside of society that made viewers wary of big cities and young people.

In the 1970s, terrorism became another danger to be added to everyday fears. Palestinian guerillas hijacked airplanes and disrupted the 1972 Olympics by kidnapping and killing Israeli athletes in Munich, Germany. The Irish Republican Army stepped up its violence against the British in a continuing struggle to obtain independence for Northern Ireland. West Germany witnessed kidnappings and shootouts with the Baader-Meinhof gang. "What we want to do and show," Ulrike Meinhof told a reporter, "is that armed confrontation is feasible. . . . Cops have to be fought as representatives of the system."

The truth is that the world then was in an uproar. In 1963, President Kennedy was assassinated. In 1968, two more of America's great leaders, Martin Luther King Jr., the leader of America's civil rights movement, and Robert F. Kennedy, brother of the fallen president and himself a presidential candidate, were felled by assassins' bullets. Across the world, in Vietnam, over half a million U.S. troops were involved in a war that divided America. So even though we tend to imagine that life several decades ago was much more peaceful and restrained than now, the truth is that the world then was in greater turmoil than today.

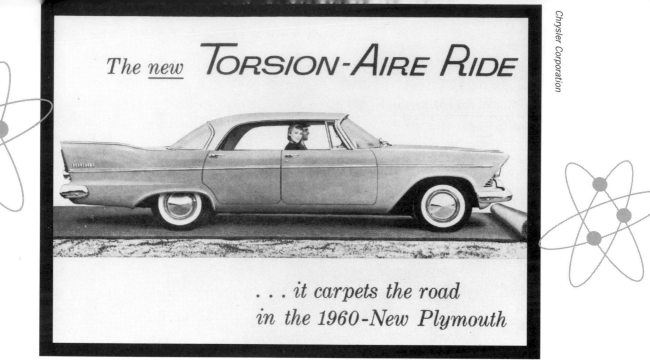

The *new* TORSION-AIRE RIDE

... *it carpets the road in the 1960-New Plymouth*

⑥ See the USA in Your Chevrolet

Today, with our highways clogged, people are urged to commute to work by public transportation or car pools. On a daily basis, near gridlock occurs on the roads leading to and from America's cities. Yet most drivers have little choice but to join the long lines of traffic. Public transportation is neither convenient nor accessible for many. So the traffic jams continue along with the pollution from automobile emissions.

It didn't have to be so. The National System of Interstate and Defense Highways that evolved during the 1950s changed the entire fabric of the country. Other forms of transportation fell into disrepair and disfavor. Trolley lines, which for decades had provided efficient service, disappeared from American cities. Commuter trains and bus lines had their schedules cut back. The automobile industry was then the most powerful political lobby in Washington, DC. Together with other auto-related businesses such as garages, motels, highway restaurants, and tourism, this lobby successfully influenced government decisions to add miles of new superhighways while drastically cutting funds to mass transportation.

In February 1994, the American Society of Civil Engineers declared the interstate highway system one of the "seven wonders of the United States."

There were positive aspects to vast highway construction. The Interstate Highway Act of 1956 was the largest public works project in American history. When completed, its 43,000 miles linked together all parts of the country with ribbons of well-maintained and constructed highways.

During the 1950s, Detroit kept producing ever-larger automobiles, presenting new concerns for safety. Inside, during the

In 1919 the United States Army sent a caravan of sixty military vehicles across the country to see how long it would take. Starting out from Washington, DC, the convoy reached San Francisco sixty-two days later. The young army officer in charge was Lt. Colonel Dwight David Eisenhower. Twenty-five years later, as Supreme Commander of allied troops in Europe during World War II, General Eisenhower marveled at the well-maintained network of highways the German enemy had built to enable them to move troops and armor easily throughout their country. When he became president in 1952, Eisenhower pushed for the construction of a modern national highway system. The "National System of Interstate and Defense Highways" was one of the most successful government projects. The complexity of the project is evident in this photograph from Los Angeles. It created thousands of jobs. But in some areas, particularly cities, construction of the new massive highways literally altered the face of established communities and businesses. Although the System contains less than 5 percent of the country's four million miles of public roads, it carries over 40 percent of America's highway traffic and 70 percent of the nation's truck traffic. Today, 90 percent of all Americans live within five miles of a System road. Speaking on the occasion of the Highway System's fiftieth anniversary, Vice President Al Gore said, "The National Highway System has dramatically stimulated commerce . . . changed the way we lived and the way we worked . . . given our nation the freedom of mobility . . . and has done more to bring Americans together than any other law in our history."
National Archives

> In 1985, U.S. residents traveled on a total of 301 million trips. That number increased to 434 million in 1995.
>
> —U.S. Bureau of the Census, *Statistical Abstract*

summer months, passengers felt the heat. Although automobile air-conditioning first appeared in 1953, it took well over a decade until it became a popular addition to most cars. Driving an automobile required greater effort—and skill—since most vehicles came with standard shifts. Automatic transmission did not become widely available until the late 1950s.

The manufacturers utilized every tool of modern advertising to influence buyers. Often, the ads focused on status. "The new Packard is designed to reflect your pride in the finest," one ad shouted for a brand of auto no longer manufactured. By the late 1950s, some consumers began to think that perhaps big was not the answer. Crowded highways created aggravation for drivers, as did the increased difficulty in finding parking spaces. When the Volkswagen, a tiny import from Germany, began making inroads into the sale of automobiles, the manufacturers in Detroit grudgingly decided it was time to think small. "If the public wants to lower its standard of living by driving a cheap, crowded car, we'll make it," one automobile executive said.[1]

Detroit's halfhearted early entry into the small-car market was the Chevrolet Corvair. The car was later immortalized as

The Corvair was the automobile made infamous by consumer crusader Ralph Nader in his book *Unsafe at Any Speed*. In an attempt to overcome the image of producing only large, tail-finned, gas-guzzling cars, America's big-three auto manufacturers, General Motors, Ford, and Chrysler, began to experiment with smaller cars by the late 1950s. The Corvair was a product of imaginative engineering. But, in an attempt to save money, the engineers cut the size of the tires and eliminated the stabilizing bar from the suspension system. The small tires and missing stabilizing bar put the car in danger of overturning at high speed. By the mid-1960s over one hundred lawsuits had been filed by drivers injured in Corvair accidents. After ten years of production, General Motors ended production of the Corvair in 1969. *Library of Congress*

The Volkswagen "Beetle" *(top right)* was the best-selling car in automotive history. It was designed in Germany in the 1930s to be affordable by typical families. With the conclusion of World War II, the car was imported into the United States and became popular with young and old alike because of its engineering simplicity and economical price. In 1997 Volkswagen introduced a new "Beetle" *(bottom right)*. Although similar in appearance to the older model, it was completely re-engineered to today's safety and performance standards.
Volkswagen of America

a safety hazard in Ralph Nader's book *Unsafe at Any Speed.* Corvair sales dropped over 90 percent, and Nader suddenly found himself the undisputed leader of a consumer crusade. Consumers searched out the best value for their money. They did not want to put up with shoddy or unsafe products. Back in 1956, a General Motors executive said that only "squares" wanted safe cars. He misjudged the American public. Today's automobiles are safer and America's drivers have fewer accidents than in earlier decades.

You may hear people complain about today's prices for everyday products. They sometimes forget the great technical advances that actually make these products better values. Automobile tires are a good example. Today's steel-belted radial tires are safer than the older four-ply cotton-belted models. They also last ten times longer, which actually makes them cost less per mile than tires bought thirty years ago.

> The last stoplight on the Interstate system was removed in the 1980s. It was on I-90 in Wallace, Idaho, and when it was removed, the local townspeople gave it a proper burial in the local cemetery, complete with a 21-gun salute.
>
> —Federal Highway Administration

It was only in the 1950s that major advances in automobile design led to automatic transmission, power brakes, padded dashboards, and triple-ply shatterproof windshields. While automobiles of just a few decades ago were planned to wear out quickly, today's autos are better made and better warrantied by manufacturers.

When people think nostalgically of the enjoyable times they shared in the past, they may not know that Americans have never had as much leisure time as they currently do. Over the past few decades, workers have spent less time at work and have had more time for themselves. Today, taking into account the natural population increase, there are more adult softball teams, bowling leagues, home swimming pools, and millions more golfers than in 1970. Each year, thousands of additional American families "hit the road" in home-sized recreational vehicles to tour historic and vacation sites.

Before the jet age, air travel was a more leisurely, slower, and expensive experience. Travelers often dressed in their finest clothes to fly; food service was often lavish. Air travel was primarily for the wealthy. National Archives

They spend less time getting from here to there, too. Air travel was revolutionized on October 27, 1958, when Mamie Eisenhower, wife of the president, smashed a bottle filled with water from the seven seas on the fuselage of a Pan American Boeing 707, officially ushering the United States into the commercial jet aircraft age.

With all that extra free time, Americans are definitely not spending more time doing housework and chores. According to a study by the Federal Reserve Bank of Dallas, Texas, the average American in 1950 spent four hours and twelve minutes a day doing housework; by 1990, that figure was down to three hours and thirty minutes.

When was the last time you listened to a record player, used a typewriter or adding machine, sent a telegram, or made a call on a rotary telephone? For most of the twentieth century, these machines were in common usage. Today, we take for granted and enjoy the benefits of products that did not exist when your parents or grandparents were growing up. Visits to the supermarket

The telephone of the 1950s was the rotary dial model shown here. It was originally available only in black. The introduction of touchtone dialers in the 1960s led to advances in telephone communications. Today, modems and fax machines are but two of the many new uses of telephone networks in our lives. Property of AT&T Archives. Reprinted with permission of AT&T.

are faster through the use of laser-based bar-code readers. Airplane trips are safer because of computer systems in the air and on the ground. And aren't you happy that pocket calculators are not only inexpensive, but welcome in schools? (Until recently, many teachers would not allow them in their classrooms!) We all benefit from major technological advances that improve our health and safety and bring fun into our lives.

With the conclusion of World War II, a new communications age dawned, fostered in large part by technological advances begun during the war. Until the 1960s, long-distance telephoning was considered a luxury. People really needed special reasons for calling. Today, we rarely give a second thought to calling friends and relatives nationwide. In the 1950s, there was one telephone for every three people, and a ten-minute long-distance call between New York City and Los Angeles cost the equivalent of about $60.00 in today's money. Today, such a call

> Number of overseas telephone calls (in millions):
>
> | 1980 | 1995 |
> | --- | --- |
> | 200 | 31,713 |
>
> The number of telegraph companies in business in 1980 was eight; by 1995, only two remained.
>
> Source: U.S. Bureau of the Census, Statistical Abstract

can be made for less than $3.00 from one of several telephones found in the average American home. And even as it is easier to make a long-distance call today, the quality of that call is greatly improved by fiber-optic cables, which also greatly expanded the number of calls that could be simultaneously made throughout the country. Back then, making a long-distance call involved the assistance of telephone operators and took minutes to set up. Today, we can dial the numbers ourselves and place the call within seconds.

The recent growth in the use of cellular telephones has made it possible for calls to be made and received from nearly anywhere. No wires are needed. In 1962, *Telstar*, the first communications satellite, was put into orbit, making it easier to transmit telephone calls and radio and television programs over wide distances. Today, satellites high above the earth routinely process everything from live news

Television technology has advanced greatly in the past fifty years. The simple, small-screen black-and-white set has given way to larger screen size, color picture, and stereo sound. Televisions today are also more reliable and cost less. *Library of Congress*

events to data transmission to telephone calls. Satellite dishes on the ground receive the data and transmit it to televisions, computers, and telephones in homes and businesses. In 1995, there were more than thirty million privately owned satellite dishes worldwide, compared with only eight million as recently as 1991.

No single invention has had such an impact on families as television. "If the television craze continues," said Boston University president Daniel Marsh in 1951, "we are destined to have a nation of morons."[2] Well, the television craze did continue, but its effect on our intelligence is not as clear. In the early days, families had access to a limited number of channels that were available only in black and white. Today, we can receive news and entertainment almost instantaneously from all over the world. Satellites link every country on earth. The Internet brings breaking news to our computer screens. The television networks in the 1950s and early 1960s limited broadcast news to nightly fifteen-minute programs. These programs were no more than radio news programs that showed the broadcaster on the screen along with occasional film clips flown in to the New York studios.

Households with:	1970	1995
Cable TV	12.6%	62.4%
VCRs	00.0%	79.0%
Color TV	47.0%	93.0%

Source: U.S. Bureau of the Census, *Statistical Abstract*

Not so long ago, people often saw news film in theaters weeks after an event. But in 1951, the coronation of Queen Elizabeth II of England was filmed and shown within days at movie theaters across America. Harry S Truman was the first American president to address the nation on television from the White House. Eight years later, Dwight D. Eisenhower became the first president to allow his news conferences to be filmed for later broadcast. Videotape was not in widespread use until the 1970s.

During an early demonstration of an experimental color television system in 1949, David Sarnoff, the president of the Radio Corporation of America (RCA), jokingly said, "The monkeys were green, the bananas were blue, and everyone had a good laugh."[3] The technical quality of today's television reception is certainly much better. The choices of what to watch have also improved, if not in quality, at least in quantity. There are many channel choices on regular television, and cable systems increase the number. In 1975, only 20 percent of American homes were connected to a cable system; by the mid-1990s, that number had grown to over 60 percent.

Television has totally changed the way we look at the world. It has allowed us to share important moments as a single nation. When events surrounding the assassination and funeral of John F. Kennedy in 1963 were broadcast live to a grieving country, Americans everywhere were linked together as a family. Today, almost anyone who was an adult back then can recount with absolute detail what television brought into their homes.

When people complain about violence and low standards on television today,

In the 1950s America fell in love with the television quiz shows. At the peak of the era, there were over twenty such shows broadcast each week. The premiere quiz show was *The $64,000 Question*. Here, Marine Captain Richard McCutchen and his father and adviser, Retired Navy Captain John C. McCutchen, congratulate each other seconds after collaborating to win the top prize, $64,000. Unknown to viewers, the show's producers often provided more popular contestants with answers to the questions. The quiz show era fell apart with the popular show *Twenty One*, when an eminent scholar, Charles van Doren, was given answers to questions he would be asked. His opponent, Herbert Stempel, was told to answer a question incorrectly. When an angered Stempel revealed the sordid details of the "fix" to investigators, a national scandal erupted. The scandal became the subject of a 1994 movie, *Quiz Show. Library of Congress*

they often speak nostalgically of the family-oriented programs of the fifties and sixties. Actually, there were more violence-oriented programs back then, including a wide variety of nightly shootings on popular police, private investigator, and rugged western shows. In fact, for a long time, gun battles, fistfights, and violent car chases highlighted the most popular programs. In reality, the number of violence-prone programs has actually dropped by nearly half since the 1970s.

From the moment Bell Laboratories unveiled the transistor in

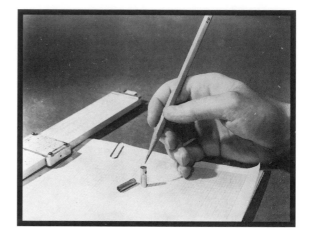

The transistor *(beneath the pencil point)*, invented in 1948 by scientists at the Bell Telephone Laboratories, quickly replaced vacuum tubes. Its transformation into miniaturized microchip technology makes possible many applications in modern technology not even dreamed about in 1948. The slide rule *(left)* was replaced for computation by handheld calculators which were not only more accurate but faster to use. *Library of Congress*

1947, technology has never been the same. The small piece of silicon replaced the bulky and fickle vacuum tubes that were needed to make televisions, radios, and

ENIAC, developed at the University of Pennsylvania in 1946, was the first working computational computer. Its uses were limited and subject to failures in its 18,000 vacuum tubes. It could perform only one function at a time. It required the space of a large room. *IBM*

early computers work. Teenagers during that decade were finally able to carry music with them wherever they went as the first battery-powered transistorized radio was offered for sale. The transistor shrunk not only the size of radios, but the price as well.

Today, not only have transistors been shrunk to microscopic size, they cost only a fraction of a penny to make and are found in a wide variety of useful machines. They help run automobile engines, microwave ovens, electronic toys, military weapons, fax machines, photocopiers, and cellular telephones. When tubes were replaced by transistors in computers, the result was an immediate increase in their use in business, resulting in lower prices and increased reliability.

The first fully electronic computer was the ENIAC (Electronic Numerical Integrator and Computer), invented at the University of Pennsylvania. It weighed 30 tons and contained 18,000 vacuum tubes, which failed on a regular basis. The average personal computer found today in homes and schools is smaller and more powerful than the early giants, at a fraction of the price.

In the 1960s and 1970s, the personal computer was first used as "a fancy calculator." As the technology improved, computers increased their importance in business and government as processors of statistical data, organizers of inventories, and overseers of accounting functions. The era of word processing was born in 1976 when Wang Computers introduced the first computerized word processor at a cost of $30,000 each. Developer An Wang said, "People saw text editing done on a screen and they thought it was magic."[4] In 1977, the Apple II personal computer was introduced. Within three years, over 120,000 were sold. IBM entered the market with its own system in 1981. By 1985, over ten million personal computers were found in offices. The technology benefited every industry. Newspapers, for example, could do away with time-consuming setting of type by composing articles directly on computer terminals. The age of desktop publishing was born.

Steve Jobs and Steve Wozniak formed the Apple Computer Company in 1976.

The PDP-8 was the first minicomputer. It marked a major step in computer downsizing, making it appropriate for small business and educational use. Developed by Digital, it appeared in 1965, the result of miniaturization of the integrated circuit which contained thousands of transistors on a small silicon chip. *Smithsonian Institution*

The evolution of the desktop home computer has led to machines with much more power than the ENIAC, able to perform increasingly complicated functions at a fraction of the cost. Shrinking circuits led to the eventual placement of the electronic insides of a computer onto a handful of small chips *IBM*

Satellite communications were unknown back in the 1950s and 1960s. Although Sputnik in 1957 was the first satellite in space, it did nothing but a emit a beep. Today, a network of artificial satellites circle the earth beaming back telephone messages, television programming, weather data, and geographic information. In 1955 there were more than thirty million satellite dishes worldwide to receive the messages beamed from space. Here, the INTELSAT V spacecraft is shown being enclosed in a protective shroud for transport. It is the largest and highest capacity commercial communications satellite built to date in 1980. *NASA*

We almost take the modern computer and its functions for granted these days. But not so long ago, much of the work now done so quickly and efficiently by computers was done by hand at a much slower pace. Even when computers became more common, they required sophisticated preparation to do their assigned chores. "Do not fold, spindle, or mutilate" became watchwords for a generation of people who were dependent on "punch cards" to input information into the massive computers. In order for the early mainframe computers to work, data had to be punched into cards—a typical program required thousands of cards—which were then fed into the computer. One mistake and the process had to be repeated.

The automobile industry was among the first to make use of microprocessors—the "brains" of a computer. Engineers discov-

Texas Instruments invented the first handheld electronic calculator in 1967.

ered ways to build electronic engine-control devices to monitor speed, oxygen content, and exhaust emissions. The 1977 Oldsmobile Toronado was the first automobile with a microprocessor-controlled engine. For the first time, the proper mix of fuel and air was determined by computers to permit each automobile to optimize power, minimize pollution, and operate economically.

IBM

"To seek out new life and civilizations." That was the mission of the starship *Enterprise*. First airing in 1966, *Star Trek* was not at first a popular series. Only years later, in reruns, did it become the most widely watched and imitated science-fiction series on television. At a time when the exploration of space captured headlines, the series highlighted the commonality of all peoples. Here, we see *Star Trek* characters Dr. McCoy, Captain Kirk, and Mr. Spock. At the bottom, the spaceship *Enterprise* soars through the universe. *National Archives*

Credit cards, bank ATMs (automatic teller machines), industrial robots, fax machines, and photocopiers have had a dramatic effect on the way we live and work. In 1969, the U.S. Department of Defense opened a computer network called Arpanet to link four research universities. By 1980, Arpanet had grown to a network of four hundred host computers with access for ten thousand people. By the early 1990s, this network had transformed itself into the Internet, with worldwide access to millions of users. Information, electronic mail, and specialized bulletin boards were available to anyone with access to a computer. Today, instead of corresponding by regular mail with just a handful of friends, we can have dozens of e-mail contacts. Thanks to the development of handheld satellite telephones, no one need be out of touch in case of emergency. From the top of Mount Everest to the middle of the Sahara Desert, the world is no more than a convenient phone call away.

Millions of workers "telecommute," that is, work at their home computers miles away from the office. This is a particular benefit to men and women with young children. "I use part of my house time for work, part of my work time for the house," one working mother said.[5] For the country's physically challenged, the computer has been nothing less than a liberating tool, permitting

"Someday, man will walk on the moon," teachers told students in the 1950s. By the 1970s, that bit of wishful thinking had become an astonishing reality. Here in this 1971 photograph, Astronaut David R. Scott is shown saluting beside the United States flag on the moon. *NASA*

In this computer-generated representation, a United States space shuttle is shown docking with the International Space Station. *NASA*

them to work freely and communicate. For paralyzed people, it provides a link to the outside world and allows them to be independent. For those unable to speak, it is a voice.

Technology has come a long way in the past fifty years: from fountain pens to ballpoint pens; from bulky black rotary telephones to satellite communications and beyond. But people sometimes find it difficult to separate popular myth from reality. In his acceptance speech before the Republican National Convention in 1996, presidential candidate Senator Robert Dole said, "To those who say it was never so, that America has not been better, I say 'you're wrong,' and I know because I was there."

What will you tell your grandchildren?

An elderly man feeds pigeons in Lafayette Park in Washington, DC.
Library of Congress

⑦ We Respected Our Elders

The image persists: Grandma in her rocking chair, Grandpa looking for his false teeth. Aging has a dramatically different face in today's America. Unlike their own parents and grandparents, older people now are living longer than ever before, many well into their eighties and nineties. For most elderly citizens, that means a healthier and more enjoyable life than their parents had. They have more money, are more vocal, and are better organized. Spending doesn't stop at retirement, and older people, aged sixty-five to seventy-four, spend more per person on food, housing, transportation, and health care than younger men and women.[1] At the same time, their educational level has made older Americans more knowledgeable and sophisticated consumers who expect more information about product benefits before making a purchase.[2]

Today, less than 5 percent of all American elderly live in nursing homes. *Library of Congress*

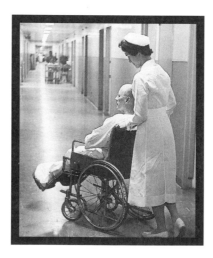

Library of Congress

When the United States was founded in 1776, life expectancy at birth stood at only about thirty-five years. It reached forty-seven years in 1900, jumped to sixty-eight years in 1950, and steadily rose to seventy-six years in 1991.[3] In fact, people aged eighty-five and above make up the fastest-growing group of the population in the United States.

"We are living not only longer but apparently better and certainly healthier," said Dr. John W. Rowe, president of the Mount Sinai School of Medicine in New York.[4] Older Americans are getting healthier for a number of reasons. They are smoking less, are better able to control high blood pressure with medication, and use aspirin to prevent heart attacks and strokes. For most of their later lives, older Americans do not experience significant physical or mental diminishment. Nearly 90 percent of people aged sixty-five to seventy-four report no disabilities, and of those over eighty-five, more than 40 percent are fully independent.

Yet as people age, they are more prone to accidents, illnesses, or decreasing mental abilities. In the later decades of life, there may be more people who face such conditions as arthritis, diabetes, osteoporosis, and mental illness. As a result, these people become dependent on others to help them perform the basic functions of daily life. Half of people over the age of eighty-five need help with at least one daily activity such as

dressing, taking medications correctly, paying bills, or telephoning. Years ago, older people had no option but to live with their families where such help was always available but at the price of burdening the younger generation.

As people live longer because of better nutrition, medical advances, and improved economic conditions, an increasing number of elderly Americans choose to continue living in their own homes. They are able to do so because of the home health care services not available even thirty years earlier. "Americans who need long-term care have more choices today," said Donna E. Shalala, the secretary of the U.S. Department of Health and Human Services. "Many more are able to stay in their homes and still receive the care they need."[5]

Mary Cole (not her real name) lives in Boston, Massachusetts. At age eighty-nine, she lives by herself. Yet, without the daily help of others, she would have to enter a nursing home. Each day, a home health aide helps the older woman dress, bathe, and shop. Near noon a meal delivery system brings a hot, nutritious meal to her door. In earlier times, these services were available only to the wealthiest Americans.

For a growing number of people who can't manage to live by themselves, assisted living provides a homelike setting with twenty-four-hour security. Frail elderly people can live with dignity knowing that their medical and social needs are readily met under one roof. A typical facility provides each resident with a small apartment, three meals a day in a common dining room, and, most importantly, personalized help with cleaning, laundry, and medications. The cost of living in such a facility is high, but governmental and private nonprofit agencies are exploring ways of making assisted living affordable for more people.

In the long run, supporting elderly persons in assisted

Library of Congress

Elderhostel

living facilities or in their own homes is preferable to the traditional placement in nursing homes. Indeed, there has been a declining occupancy in nursing homes over the last few decades. Since 1985, the number of nursing home residents was up only 4 percent despite an 18 percent increase in the population aged sixty-five and over. In 1996, people over the age of sixty-five represented nearly 13 percent of the American population. That figure is expected to double by the year 2030.

Today, older Americans are involved in more activities than a generation ago. Many continue to work, others take courses at local universities, while still others keep busy as volunteers in schools and social service agencies. An increasingly popular activity is the Elderhostel program, which offers accomodations and short courses or educational experiences for senior citizens. Each year, thousands of men and women travel to different parts of the country for university courses, archaeological digs, and other cultural experiences.

Elderhostel

Over 90 percent of older Americans depend on Social Security as their major source of income. Proposed in 1935 by President Franklin D. Roosevelt, the Social Security Act provided older Americans with a minimum monthly retirement check. Over the years, the system grew to encompass more people, but the payments were small and many elderly had a hard time financially. Lacking from the Social Security system was any provision for health care, perhaps the greatest need of America's older citizens.

The Elderhostel program, begun in 1975 with 220 participants, enrolled over 323,000 elderly people in 1996 in its educational and travel programs.

Dramatic changes happened in 1965 when President Lyndon Johnson signed the Medicare bill into law to provide medical coverage for nineteen million older Americans. Prior to the bill's enactment, half of all elderly citizens had no health insurance. When illness struck, many were driven into poverty. Before 1965, only 56 percent of the elderly had hospital insurance. Today, nearly all American senior citizens are insured by Medicare, the nation's largest health insurer. In addition, Medicare also covers four million disabled Americans under the age of sixty-five and over two hundred thousand with life-threatening kidney disease, enabling them to receive health services many could not otherwise afford.

> In 1970, 20.5 million elderly were enrolled in the Medicare program. In 1995, that number had grown to 36.9 million.
>
> Source: U.S. Bureau of the Census, Statistical Abstract

Medicare improved the elderly's access to health care and their quality of life and has significantly contributed to improving the health status of older Americans. As a result of greater access to medical care through Medicare, the risk of death from heart disease and stroke has decreased dramatically in the last three decades. Nearly three years have been added to the life expectancies of sixty-five-year-old Americans since Medicare was enacted. In addition, Medicare's support of home health care for the ill and hospice services to help comfort the dying has enabled patients to be treated in their homes. These services, which did not widely exist thirty years ago, have removed from families the burden of physically caring for elderly relatives. These services are less expensive than hospitalization and add dignity to the medical treatment of the

January 7, 1965—Thirty years ago, the American people made a basic decision that the later years of life should not be years of despondency and drift. The result was enactment of our Social Security program. . . . Since World War II, there has been increasing awareness of the fact that the full value of Social Security would not be realized unless provision were made to deal with the problem of costs of illnesses among our older citizens. . . . Compassion and reason dictate that this logical extension of our proven Social Security system will supply the prudent, feasible, and dignified way to free the aged from the fear of financial hardship in the event of illness.

—President Lyndon B. Johnson, as he presented former President Harry S Truman with the first Medicare Card

This picture from the 1960s is not representative of the conditions which existed back then for the physically challenged in America. For people who used wheelchairs, getting around was sometimes impossible. There were few if any wheelchair cuts in sidewalks, specially built restrooms, or public transportation access. There have been great changes in the 1990s with the enactment and enforcement of strict rules regarding accessibility for handicapped people. *National Archives*

elderly. The poverty rate among the elderly has declined from 29 percent, when Medicare began, to 12 percent today. Medicare and increased Social Security benefits act as "safety nets" to protect a large proportion of the elderly.

The Medicare program was signed into law at a time when African Americans were denied basic rights in many parts of the United States. One of Medicare's primary policies was to abolish discrimination against minorities. Medical facilities that did not comply with the government's antidiscriminatory policy would be unable to participate in the Medicare program.

The elderly were also helped by the passage in 1990 of the Americans with Disabilities Act. The act provided protection for all Americans, including senior citizens, against discrimination in employment, public accomodations, transportation, and communication. In other ways, the federal government has taken an active role in meeting the needs of older persons and their families. The Nutrition Program for the Elderly, for example, provides elderly people with nutritionally sound meals through home delivery of "meals-on-wheels" or in senior citizen centers.

Through the Title IV funding program of the Older Americans Act, the Administration on Aging has sponsored projects to provide the elderly with home health care, legal services, transportation, respite care, adult day care, and many

Today, people are living longer and healthier lives thanks to advances in medicine, nutrition, and health care. Senior citizens who several decades ago would have found themselves in nursing homes continue to lead interesting and enjoyable lives. *Elderhostel*

services that did not exist just a few years earlier. There was little awareness of the problems of abuse faced by the elderly in the later 1970s and early 1980s. The Department of Justice has provided training to local law enforcement officers to help them prevent the mistreatment of older adults by family members and care-givers.

Elderly Americans today are more financially secure than ever before, and they have a poverty rate that is lower than any other part of the population. Their quality of life has been improved by the benefits derived from Medicare. Medical treatments unavailable just a few years ago are now routinely available. Removal of cataracts to improve vision, heart surgery advancements, and new medications to treat a variety of previously incurable ailments prolong life and the quality of living.

⑧ Golden Childhood

It began with a "beep, beep, beep." On October 4, 1957, at the height of the Cold War, the Soviet Union launched the world's first unmanned artificial satellite into space. *Sputnik I* weighed only 184 pounds but struck immense terror into American hearts. The United States no longer felt invincible. The Soviets, who just a few years earlier produced their own atomic bomb, demonstrated with their launch of *Sputnik* the ability to send nuclear-carrying missiles into the heart of America.

Sputnik damaged America's self-image. U.S. Senator Henry Jackson

called the satellite "a devastating blow to the prestige of the United States as the leader in the scientific and technical world."[1] A month later, when the Soviets launched the heavier *Sputnik II*, which even carried a dog aloft, an American maga-

zine warned that the entire world "might be at a turning point." Communism seemed to be on the rise. The Soviets dominated Eastern Europe and possessed a growing arsenal of nuclear weaponry. China, with its huge landmass and population, became a communist country in 1949. Americans, frightened more than ever about the threat of communist expansion and nuclear annihilation, wanted government action. Something had to be done—and done quickly—to return the United States to its unchallenged world leadership role.

Prior to the launching of *Sputnik*, little emphasis was placed on the teaching of science and mathematics in American schools. No one really thought much about space. The successful launch of *Sputnik* caused many to wonder if the United States had lost its technological superiority. President Eisenhower took advantage of the moment to promote the training of scientists and engineers. "People are alarmed and thinking about science," he said, "and perhaps this alarm could be turned toward a constructive result."[2] Admiral Hyman G. Rickover, the "father" of America's nuclear navy, said, "Let us not forget that there can be no second place in a contest with Russia and that there will be no second chance if we lose."[3] The admiral could not

The use of technology in classrooms was quite limited in the 1950s and early 1960s. A record player in the classroom and the occasional showing of an educational film defined what was available. The shock of *Sputnik* changed the look of American classrooms. The federal government allocated funds for the purchase of new audiovisual equipment and educational materials. In this picture, a teacher in Euclid, Ohio, in 1966 uses audiovisual electronic devices to help beginning pupils attain third-year reading proficiency in eight months.
National Archives

have predicted that the Soviet Union would self-destruct in 1991.

In 1958, Congress passed the National Defense Education Act (NDEA) to provide funds for college student loans and scholarships, as well as scientific equipment

Susan Di Pesa

for public and private schools. The emphasis of the NDEA was on the study of mathematics, science, and foreign languages. With the financial support of the federal government, schools began an intensive restructuring of these academic areas. For the first time in American history, the federal government became seriously involved in education, which until then had been the sole responsibility of local and state governments. In the late 1970s, the United States Department of Education was created.

Although great progress was made—new textbooks, improvement of teacher training, and more emphasis on the sciences—educational achievement was not totally successful. In 1983, a national commission on education issued its landmark report, *A Nation at Risk.* "If an unfriendly foreign power," the report said, "had attempted to impose on America the mediocre educational performance that exists today, we might well have viewed it as an act of war."[4]

Teachers in rural schools were poorly prepared through the 1960s. The school buildings were old-fashioned and ill-equipped. Courses were rarely updated. Some teachers had no understanding of their students. Physical punishment was common in schools everywhere. When a *New York Times* reporter visited a southern rural school in 1951, he recorded this conversation with a teacher:

"Do you ever use this paddle?"

"I sure do!" the teacher replied.

"Quiet!" The teacher turned to a boy of 10 or 11 and threatened, "I'll beat the daylights out of you later.

". . . Yes, sirree," the teacher continued, "the paddle keeps 'em from running all over you. You got to use every trick of the trade in this business . . . the paddle is the thing. If they don't behave just have 'em bend over and give 'em a good clip on the bucket."[5]

During the 1950s and 1960s, millions of Americans felt the results of decades of poverty and discrimination. President Johnson declared a "War on Poverty," which particularly encouraged special programs to improve the health and education of children of low-income families. Operation Head Start, one of the most successful programs, targeted preschool children from disadvantaged homes. The goal was to prepare young children for a successful school experience by improving health, nutrition, and social skills for them and their parents. Prior to this program, the first school experience for these children would have been kindergarten. By then, it was often too late to reverse deficiencies of their first few years of life.

This era also marked the beginning of *Sesame Street*, the happy and educational hour-long program that revolutionized television for children. Children's programming

Howdy Doody was television's premiere children's show. It first aired in 1947. In the early days of television, it kept children occupied in the late afternoons as mothers prepared for dinner. "Buffalo Bob" Smith and the wooden marionettes sang and performed for the children seated in the studio's "Peanut Gallery" and those at home seated in front of the small black-and-white screens. *Library of Congress*

The first *Sesame Street* program appeared on November 10, 1969. Since then, it has provided young children with a fun way to prepare for school. Its fast-paced programming combined education with entertainment. It was unlike any previous children's television show in format, appeal, and educational value. © 1998 *Children's Television Workshop/Richard Terminz. Sesame Street Muppets* © *1998 Jim Henson Productions.*

The care and education of preschool children was not a priority concern in the 1950s and early 1960s. Mothers were expected to stay home with their young children. When women began working in large numbers outside the home, the need for day care for their children was clear. Also, President Lyndon Johnson's War on Poverty specifically targeted poor, preschool-aged children to assure their educational and health preparedness for school. *Library of Congress*

prior to *Sesame Street* often lacked educational content. Perhaps the most popular show of the 1950s was *Howdy Doody*. Ask anyone who grew up during that period, "Say, kids, what time is it?" You will probably be answered immediately with an off-key version of the show's theme song, "It's Howdy Doody Time!" Beyond the nostalgia and fun, however, there was little learning. *Howdy Doody* went off the air in 1960. *Sesame Street* continues to flourish.

Today, we take for granted that children from all backgrounds may be our classmates. For handicapped children, the experience of attending school with nonhandicapped students was a rarity for much of the twentieth century. In the early 1970s, President Gerald Ford signed into law an act intended to improve opportunities in education for handicapped children.

When older people look back nostalgically upon their school experiences, they

Around 1950, television came to town and brought the phenomenon of generous neighbors, even the childless, allowing the local urchins into their living rooms to watch this entertainment miracle. I remember clearly a few minutes before 5:00 each weekday knocking on the door of the elderly couple across the street. They welcomed me in, and I sat transfixed in front of the portholelike screen of the Dumont set and watched the grainy black-and-white shows. First, *Freddy Freihofer* in which a man with a grease crayon (no Magic Markers in those days) drew on an easel the adventures of the large-eyed, long-eared trademark of the Freihofer Baking Company. I can still hear the theme song. Then, of course, it was time for *Howdy Doody* and another memorable song and characters. I suppose I must have been gently sent home when they wanted peace but promptly turned up again the next day.

—Carolyn Bishop

remember discipline, lack of violence, strict standards, and "good" education. They seem to forget that their classes usually contained more than thirty students sitting in rows of bolted-down desks and chairs. School discipline problems were handled directly. If a student was above the legal maximum age for compulsory education, he or she simply would be expelled. Naturally, the 1950s saw a rise in school dropouts and a comparable rise in the rate of juvenile delinquency.

High school graduation rates have gradually risen over the past century, from an astonishing 3 percent to about 85 percent today.

Microcomputers for student instruction in elementary and secondary schools:

	1984-1985	1996-1997
No. of students per computer	63	8

Source: U.S. Bureau of the Census, *Statistical Abstract*

Until the late 1960s, girls were missing from many high school science and mathematics courses—they were relegated to home economics and business subjects. Discriminatory regulations kept many schools segregated by race even after the Supreme Court's 1954 decision in *Brown v. the Board of Education* overturned the prevailing practice of separate but equal. *Separate* meant that whites and blacks were kept apart, particularly in the South. *Equal*, in effect, meant not equal.

"The teenagers of today are stronger, smarter, more self-sufficient, and more constructive than any other generation of teenagers in history."

—Herman G. Stark, Director of the State of California Youth Authority, 1958

In the 1950s, people who completed the eighth grade could easily find employment in factories of the "smokestack industries." For many, attending high school was an extravagance; college, out of the question. When the factories became obsolete and began to close, or move to other countries where wages were lower, workers with little education were the first to feel the economic crunch. As educational quality improved, students could become skilled workers and also better consumers who could understand the benefits of a new product before making a purchase. The number of students heading off to college today is nearly two and a half times what it was thirty years ago. Today's college students arrive at their dormitory rooms better

The face of America is more diverse today than ever. Students in the 1950s and 60s had fewer opportunities to meet children from different races, religions, and backgrounds. *Susan Di Pesa*

equipped than their parents. A *Boston Globe* reporter listed the typical contents of a dorm room today: television, video-cassette recorder, stereo, microwave oven, telephone with answering machine, and a refrigerator. When he went to college, he wrote, he brought with him two appliances: a heater to warm his coffee and a clock radio.[6]

Public schools are beginning to prepare students to take on the new jobs and changing technology. In the 1950s and early 1960s, many schools "tracked" their students into course choices and careers based on the students' social positions and family background. African American students were routinely put on a low track, making it difficult to obtain a decent education. Most black high school students in 1953 dropped out of school. A few went on to college. Today, a third of all African American high school graduates go on to attend college. Forty to fifty years ago, segregated schools for African Americans were overcrowded, and in many cases, the textbooks used were cast-offs from local white high schools. No one could ever have imagined that by the 1990s, there would be African Americans in Congress and in other leadership positions in the government and the military.

The era of the use of computers in education, which we take for granted today, is little more than thirty-five years old. In 1963, fewer than 1 percent of high schools in the United States used computers for instructional purposes. By the late 1970s, computers were no longer a luxury but a necessity. Today, mil-

Teacher-to-pupil ratio:

1960	1996 (projected)
1:26.4	1:17.1

Source: U.S. Bureau of the Census, *Statistical Abstract*

lions of users are tied into thousands of networks with connections to the Internet. At the same time, the number of books published annually in the United States has almost doubled since 1965!

Who were Dick and Jane? Just ask someone who learned to read in the forties, fifties, or sixties. For thirty years, the "Dick and Jane" books were the most popular elementary school textbooks. In the series, Dick and Jane lived in a perfect and idealized world with their two parents, a baby sister named Sally, a kitten named Puff, and their dog, Spot. "See Spot run" was one of the best-known sentences in print. Father, who worked in an office, wore a suit, tie, and hat even while taking the family for a ride in the country. Mother, who was a homemaker, swept the front stairs wearing a frilly dress. The family never noticed the events of the real world: the traffic jams, the wars, the fear of nuclear attack, or the anti-Vietnam demonstrations. By the 1970s, the model family disappeared from textbooks. In their place came a large number of new books that more realistically depicted America at midcentury.

Sally said, "Oh, Tim.
I see something.
Mother sees something.
Dick and Jane see something."

The "Dick and Jane" readers were widely used in schools during the 1950s. They depicted the life of a happy suburban family. While millions of children learned to read with the help of these popular books, the contents did little to teach about the "real" world. *Addison Wesley Educational Publishers, Inc.*

If lunch is the favorite school activity for most students, complaining about the cafeteria food must be second. "Nothing is more important in our national life," President Truman said, referring to the 1946 congressional passage of the National School Lunch Act,

Susan Di Pesa

"than the welfare of our children, and proper nutrition comes first in attaining this welfare." Until then, the availability of nutritious meals was haphazard around the country. The typical school meal has changed dramatically over the years.

Its beginnings were an attempt to encourage increased consumption of the country's agricultural surpluses of milk, cheese, meats, and vegetables. The positive benefit was "to safeguard the health and well-being of the nation's children." Carefully structured rules mandated the use of certain foods such as butter and whole milk. Today, cafeteria food is not only tastier, but better for you. Our parents and grandparents were only given whole, full-fat milk. Now school lunches include healthy choices of low-fat or skim milk and margarine. Until 1976, there was a federal requirement that butter, high in fat content, had to be served with every meal.

By the mid-1960s, the program was expanded to include school breakfast. Today, school meals continue to change to reflect new nutritional knowledge and the relationship between diet and health. One food-service director recalled that back in the 1960s "there wasn't much creativity, but the students were less sophisticated then and were easier to please."[7]

Until well into the 1980s, girls' participation in sports was often limited to cheering boys' teams on to victory. Today, schools are required to offer girls equal sports opportunities to what is available to boys. *Susan Di Pesa*

School sports too have changed dramatically over the past decades. In 1972, less than 8 percent of all high school athletes were girls. That year, Title IX of the Education Amendment of 1972 of the 1964 Civil Rights Act law was passed by Congress to prohibit sex discrimination at any educational institution that receives federal aid. Today, 40 percent of college athletes are women.

The world is a more complicated and sophisticated place than it was just a generation or two earlier. Today's students reflect those changes in their lives at home and at school and are more aware of the world around them.

Epilogue

Are the "good old days" a myth? Sometimes, myths become more accepted than true history. The facts, according to *Time* magazine, are that "right now, on a day you are lucky to be alive to see, the U.S. is enjoying its best economic and social health in 25 years. We're living longer, breathing cleaner air, drinking cleaner water. Crime is in free fall, with violent evildoing near a 22-year low, and the downtowns we once gave up for dead are bristling with coffee bars, green markets, life."[1]

In addition, the article continues, "Poverty rates for elderly and black Americans are at their lowest levels since Washington began keeping track of such matters in 1959. Welfare rolls are shrinking, and though too many human beings are falling destitute as a result, many others are being forced to remake their lives for the better. People who haven't held a job in years are rediscovering the sense of self-worth that working brings."[2]

Think of the helpful technology that did not exist back then. There are new drugs and medical tests unknown to our parents and grandparents. CD players bring brilliant music to our ears by way of portable players we can take to the beach. We can make cellular phone calls from nearly anywhere with telephones that easily fit in our pockets. We play games and learn the alphabet with electronic devices that cost under $30.00. And if parents need money to buy those technological marvels for their children, they can go to the ATM around the corner at any time of the day or night to withdraw cash.

Although the world is still beset with many problems, life is getting better for most people. The Cold War, which kept the world on the edge of nuclear war, is over. The environment is not as polluted as it once was. We are healthier, safer, and live longer than ever before.

Times change. Yet, in spite of nostalgic views of the past, each generation makes its own mark on our culture with its unique successes and problems. Today, we have so many choices it sometimes becomes difficult to choose wisely. Information bombards us like never before to the point where most of us suffer from information overload. That presents us with the special responsibility to make appropriate choices and use all our freedoms intelligently. Society has always built upon the memories and accomplishments of our parents and grandparents. What great deeds are you going to leave for the next generation?

NOTES

Chapter 1
1. Kehret, Peg, *Small Steps: The Year I Got Polio*. Morton Grove, IL: Whitman, 1996, pp. 44–45.
2. Stanton, Pamela, "Polio and the Era of Fear," Lincolnshire Post-Polio Network, 1996.
3. "Dial 1-800-History," *American Heritage*, February/March 1994, p. 30.
4. "Utah Lags as U.S. Sets Record for Immunizations," *The Salt Lake Tribune*, March 2, 1997, p. 3.
5. "Vital Statistics Report Shows Significant Gain in Health," Press Release, U.S. Department of Health and Human Services, September 11, 1997.
6. Bruce C. Vladick MD, quoted in Press Release, U.S. Department of Health and Human Services, May 16, 1997.
7. "Proton Beam Targets Tumors," *ABC News*, December 4, 1997.
8. *National Wildlife*, February/March 1996.

Chapter 2
1. "Americans Have Never Had It So Good," *Consumer's Research Magazine*, October 1994, p. 28.
2. Kirsch, Barbara, "Healthy Foods, To Go," *Army and Air Force Exchange Service News*, November 1995.
3. U.S. Food and Drug Administration, "The New Food Label," FDA report. Washington, DC, May 1995.

Chapter 3
1. Browner, Carol, Speech to the Hazardous Waste World Superfund XVIII Conference, December 2, 1997.
2. Wald, Matthew L., *New York Times News Service*, July 29, 1997.
3. Eisler, Peter, and Steve Sternberg, Study: "Fallout Fell Far From Nevada Test Site," *USA Today*, July 25, 1997, p. 1.
4. Remarks by James B. Steinberg to the Carnegie Endowment for International Peace, Washington, DC, June 9, 1997.

Chapter 4
1. *New York Times*, August 7, 1959.
2. *Time*, January 5, 1976.
3. *Look*, October 16, 1956, pp. 35–42.
4. Kimbrough, Emily, "She Needs Some Years of Grace," *Life*, December 24, 1956, p. 28.
5. *Time*, May 5, 1976.

Chapter 5
1. *New York Times*, March 11, 1951, p. 23.
2. Finkelstein, Norman H., *With Heroic Truth, The Life of Edward R. Murrow*. New York: Clarion Books, 1997, p. 140.
3. Presidential News Conference, October 5, 1957.
4. Finkelstein, Norman H., *Heeding the Call*. Philadelphia: The Jewish Publication Society, 1997, p. 126.

5. *Time*, February 20, 1956, p. 47.

6. Remarks of President Bill Clinton at Central High School, Little Rock, Arkansas, September 25, 1997.

Chapter 6

1. Keats, John, *The Insolent Chariots*. Philadelphia: Lippincott, 1958.

2. *Macleans*, December 25, 1995.

3. *Popular Electronics*, July 1995, p. 55.

4. Lubar, Stephen D., *InfoCulture: The Smithsonian Book of Information Age Inventions*. Boston: Houghton Mifflin, 1993, p. 38.

5. *Time*, January 3, 1983.

Chapter 7

1. "The Ungraying of America," *American Demographics*, July 1997.

2. Franzese, Peter, "America at Mid Decade," *American Demographics*, February 1995.

3. U.S. Department of Commerce, "Sixty Five Plus in the United States." Washington, DC: Census Bureau, May 1995.

4. Foreman, Judy, "Americans Live Both Longer and Healthier," *Boston Globe*, October 17, 1997, p. A3.

5. From a U.S. Department of Health and Human Services News Release, January 23, 1997.

Chapter 8

1. "Sputnik I: the Little Satellite That Did," "Sputnik's Legacy," University of Wisconsin, 1997.

2. "Sputnik's Legacy," University of Wisconsin, 1997.

3. Rickover, Hyman, *Education and Freedom*. New York: Dutton, 1959, p. 89.

4. United States National Commission on Excellence in Education, *A Nation at Risk*. Washington, DC: The Commission, 1983, p. 144.

5. *New York Times*, March 12, 1951, p. 18.

6. Stein, Charles, "Things Are Better Than You Think," *Boston Globe*, January 5, 1997, p. 12.

7. *Food Management*, October 1997, p. 65.

Epilogue

1. *Time*, May 21, 1997, p. 29.

2. *Time*, May 21, 1997, p. 30.

FURTHER READING

Carson, Rachel. *Silent Spring*. Boston: Houghton-Mifflin, 1962.

Coontz, Stephanie. *The Way We Never Were: American Families and the Nostalgia Trap*. New York: Basic Books, 1992.

Coontz, Stephanie. *The Way We Really Are*. New York: Basic Books, 1997.

Elliott, Michael. *The Day Before Yesterday*. New York: Simon & Schuster, 1996.

Farber, David, ed. *The Sixties: From Memory to History*. Chapel Hill: University of North Carolina Press, 1994.

Finkelstein, Norman H. *Thirteen Days/Ninety Miles: The Cuban Missile Crisis*. New York: Messner/Simon & Schuster, 1994 (YA).

Finkelstein, Norman H. *With Heroic Truth: The Life of Edward R. Murrow*. New York: Clarion Books, 1997 (YA).

Harvey, Brett. *The Fifties: A Women's Oral History*. New York: Harper, 1993.

Kehret, Peg. *Small Steps: The Year I Got Polio*. Morton Grove, IL: Whitman, 1996 (YA).

Kleinfelder, Rita Lang. *When We Were Young: A Baby-Boomer Yearbook*. New York: Prentice-Hall, 1993.

Kort, Michael G. *The Cold War*. Brookfield, CT: Millbrook Press, 1994 (YA).

Lubar, Steven D. *InfoCulture: The Smithsonian Book of Information Age Inventions*. Boston: Houghton-Mifflin, 1993.

Nader, Ralph. *Unsafe at Any Speed: The Designed-In Dangers of the American Automobile*. New York: Grossman, 1965.

Oakley, J. Ronald. *God's Country: America in the Fifties*. New York: Dembner Books, 1990.

Rickover, Hyman. *Education and Freedom*. New York: Dutton, 1959.

Rubel, David. *The United States in the 20th Century*. New York: Scholastic Press, 1995 (YA).

Siegel, Beatrice. *The Year They Walked: Rosa Parks and the Montgomery Bus Boycott*. New York: Simon & Schuster, 1992 (YA).

Stark, David D. *Glued to the Set*. New York: Free Press, 1997.

U.S. Bureau of the Census. *Statistical Abstract of the United States, 1996*. (116th ed.), Washington, DC, 1996.

Walter, Mildred Pitts. *Mississippi Challenge*. New York: Simon & Schuster, 1992 (YA).

INDEX

Note: Page numbers for illustrations are in italics.

A
Accidents
      and car safety, *13*, 13-15, 65
      from nuclear power, 35
      reduction in, 13-16
Advertising
      for appliances, *45*
      for cars, *62*, 64, *64*
      for food, 21, 24-25
Air travel, *66*, 66 67
Air-conditioning, 43, 64
Army
      testing weapons, 36
      troop movements of, *63*
Assassinations, 60-61
Assisted living, for elderly, 77-78

B
Berlin, in Cold War, *48*, *49*
Brown v. the Board of Education, 87
Browner, Carol, 32

C
Cancers, 10-11, *11*
      and pollution, 29-30
      and radiation, 33-35
      from smoking, 11-13
Cars, *62*, 64-66
      computer chips in, 72
      dependence on, 62-63
      and highway system, 32-33
      pollution from, 28
      safety issues about, 13-14, 64-65
Carson, Rachel, 28
Chaney, James, 58
Children, 82-91
      and accidents, 15-16
      advertising to, 21
      of blacklisted parents, 52-53
      effects of pollution on, 31, 34-35
      and family life, 41-42
      health of, 3-8

Cities, 92
       and growth of suburbs, 43-44
       pollution in, 26-27, 30
       poverty in, *42*, 58-59
       public housing in, 45
       riots in, 58-59
Civil Defense measures, 32-33, 50-51
Civil rights
       and education, 87
       and McCarthyism, 51-53
       protests, 56-58, *59*
       and radiation experiments, 36-37
Clinton, President Bill, 37, 57
Cold War, *48, 49*, 49-51, 93
       end of, 37
       and highway system, 32-33, 63
Communism
       and Cold War, 49-51
       fear of, 50-53, 83
Computers, 68, 70-72, *70-72*
       in education, 87-89
Consumer Products Safety
Commission, 15-16
Costello, Frank, 60
Crime, 48, 59-60, 87, 92
       and public housing, 45-46

D
Day care, 85-86, *86*
Death rates, 8-9, 15
Disabilities, *80*
       and education, 86
       and Medicare, 79-80
Divorce rate, 46
Dole, Robert, 74
Drugs. *See also* Health and
medicine
       illegal, *53*, 54
       prescription, 46

E
Earth Day, 26
Education
       changes in, 86-91
       for elderly, 78
       integration of, 57-58, 87-88
       McCarthyism in, 52
       protests at universities, 54-55
       and technological advances, 82-84, *83*

for women, 47, 91
Eisenhower, Mamie, 66
Eisenhower, President Dwight, 53
    and highway system, *63*
    and integration, 57
    and Soviet Union, 83
    on TV, 69
Elderly, 75-81
    health care for, 8, 45
Emergency care, *7*, 8-9
Environmental movement, 26-37
Ethnic groups
    diversity of, *88*
    food from, 23-24

F
Factories
    and need for education, 87
    pollution from, *27*, 27-28, 30
Family life
    and commuting, 44
    eating habits, 20-21
    and elderly, 77, 79
    roles in, 39-41, 46-47
    in school books, 89
    strength of, 41-42
    and TV, 38-40, 68-70
Fast-food chains, 21-23, *22*
Food
    eating habits, 17-25, *23*
    for elderly, 77, 80
    in family life, 41-42
    and health, 8, 10
    in schools, 89-91
Ford, President Gerald, 86

G
Goodman, Andrew, 58
Gore, Vice President Al, *63*
Government, U.S.
    antipoverty programs of, 44-45, 85
    in education, 83-84
    environmental laws by, 28, 30
    in health and safety, 12-16, 24-25
    and highway system, 32-33, 50, 63
    programs for elderly, 77-81
    and school lunches, 89-91
    weapons testing by, 32-37
Grasso, Ella, 47

H

Health and medicine, 2-16, *6*
        effects of asbestos on, 29
        effects of pollution on, 28, 31
        effects of radiation on, 33-37
        and elderly, 75-76, *76*, 81
        and foods, 17-25, *23*, 90
        Medicare, 45, 79-80
Highway systems, 32-33, 50, 63, *63*, 65
Hills, Carla, 47
Hippies, *53,* 54
Hobby, Oveta Culp, 47
Homes
        elderly staying in, 77-78
        pollution in, 29
        and poverty, *42*
        public housing, 45-46
        size of, *41*, 42-43

I

Income
        of elderly, 75, 78
        satisfaction with, 39, 45
Iron lungs, 3-4, *4*

J

Jackson, Senator Henry, 83
Jobs
        education for, 87-88
        and leisure time, 66
        safety on, 15
        telecommuting, 44, 46, 73
        for women, 46-47
Johnson, President Lyndon B.
        antipoverty programs of, 44, 85
        and Medicare, 79

K

Kefauver, Estes, 59-60
Kehret, Peg, 4
Kennedy, President John F., 58
        assassination of, 60, 69
        in Cold War, *48*, 54
Kennedy, Senator Robert, 60
Kent State University, 54-55
Khrushchev, Nikita, *48*, 53
Kimbrough, Emily, 47
King, Dr. Martin Luther, Jr., *55*, 57, 60
Korean War, 50

L

Lansky, Meyer, 60
Lead, *14*, 15
Levitt, William, 44
Life expectancy, 8, 75-76, 79
Literature
      and McCarthyism, 51-52
      in schools, 89, *89*
Love Canal, 31, *32*
Lucy, Autherine, 57

M

Makhijani, Arjun, 34
Marsh, Daniel, 68
Marshall, Thurgood, *55*, 55-56
McCarthy, Senator Joseph R., 51-53, *52*
Medicare, 45, 79-80
Medicine. *See* Health and medicine
Meinhof, Ulrike, 60
Men, role in families, 41, 89
Migrant workers, 59
Minorities, *55*, *88*
      and civil rights movement, 55-59
      discrimination against, 44, 87-88
      Medicare for, 80
      on TV, 42
Money
      of elderly, 81
      and spending, 39, *45*, 75
Movies
      and McCarthyism, 51-52
      news clips at, 69
      smoking in, 12
      violence in, 60
Murrow, Casey, 53
Murrow, Edward R., 11, 53
Music
      Beatles, 40
      Elvis Presley, *41*

N

Nader, Ralph, 14, 35, 64-65
Nation at Risk, A, 84
Neighborhoods, changes in, 43-44
Nuclear power, 35, *36*
Nuclear weapons, 33, *34*, 37
      and Soviet space program, 82
      testing, 33-34, 49

O

Organized crime, 59-60

P

Parks, Rosa, 56
Perkins, Frances, 47, *47*
Plessy v. Ferguson, 56
Polio, 3-5, *5*
Politics
        environmental, 26, 29
        and McCarthyism, 51-53
        and terrorism, 60
Pollution, 26-37, 92-93
        from cars, *14*, 15
        effects of, 15, *28*
        reduction of, *31*, 32
        sources of, 15, *27*, 27-28
Poverty, 58-59, 92
        among elderly, 79-81
        and children, 85
        in cities, *42*, 43, 58-59
        programs to eliminate, *43*, 44-45
Presley, Elvis, *41*
Prices
        of car tires, 65
        of computer chips, 70
        of health care, 16
        of telephone calls, 67
Protests
        civil rights, *56-59*, 56-58
        against Vietnam War, 54-55

R

Radiation
        and Civil Defense planning, 50
        experiments with, 35-37
        from nuclear testing, 33-35
        to treat cancer, 10-11, *11*
Radio, 60
Reagan, Ronald, 34
Recreation, 66
        for elderly, 78, *78*, *80*
        sports in schools, 91
Rickover, Admiral Hyman G., 83-84
Roosevelt, President Franklin D., 78
Rowe, Dr. John W., 76

S

Sabin, Dr. Albert, 4-5

Safety
  of cars, 65
  of food, 24-25
  government in, 12-16
  and pollution, 27
Salk, Dr. Jonas, 4
Sarnoff, David, 69
Satcher, Dr. David, 7
Satellites
  communication, 67-68, *72*, 73
  monitoring pollution, 30
  in Soviet space program, 53, 82-84
Schwerner, Michael, 58
Sesame Street, *85*, 85-86
Shalala, Donna E., 77
Sharp, Susie, 47
Shopping, for food, 19-21, *20-21*
Silent Spring (Carson), 28
Smoking, 10-13, 29
Soviet Union. *See also* Cold War
  competition with, 53
  space program, 82-84
Space program, *73-74*
  Soviet Union in, 53, 82-84
Sputnik, 53, 82-84
Steinberg, James B., 37
Stevenson, Adlai, 34
Street gangs, 60
Suburbs
  effects of, 46, 58
  growth of, *43*, 43-44
Suit, Dr. Herman, 11
Sutton, Carol, 47

T
Technological advances, 66-67, 92-93
  in appliances, *45*
  in communications, 67-68, 72-74
  competition in, 82-84
  in computers, 70-74
  in entertainment, 39, 69
Telephones, 43-44, *66*
  improvements in, 67-68, 73
Television
  for children, *85*, 85-86
  effects of, 68-70
  news on, 49
  programs on, *73*
  and satellites, 38-40, *40*, 67-68, *68-69*
  violence on, 58, 60